Undeniable

Cloverleigh Farms
Series

2

Melanie Harlow

Undeniable

Cover Photography: Regina Wamba
Cover Design: Hang Le
Editing: Nancy Smay, Evident Ink
Formatting: Stacey Blake, Champagne Book Design

For all the incredible writers who attended the
Gatlinburg Madcap Retreat.
You taught me, you encouraged me, you inspired me.

Loving someone requires a leap of faith,
and a soft landing is never guaranteed.

Sarah Dessen

One

Chloe

THEN

"ARE YOU SURE?"

"Of course I'm sure," Oliver scoffed. "I've jumped off way higher roofs than this."

"Because it seems like a long way down."

He shrugged. "Maybe to someone like you."

"Like me how?"

Oliver gave me a side-eyed, shit-eating grin as he flapped his elbows and clucked like a chicken.

"Stop it!" I punched him in the arm. He knew I hated being called *chicken* or *scaredy-cat* or *baby*, or any of the other names he called me because I wasn't a fan of heights. Or the dark. Or thunderstorms. Or snakes. He was exactly the type of kid who got you to tell him your secret fears and then used them against you. "I'm not a chicken."

"So jump."

"I'm going to." I jerked my chin at him and stared down at the ground from the roof of the pole barn on my family's small farm. It was late August, hotter than blazes at four in the afternoon, and the sun had baked the mud below into a crusted, chocolate-milk-colored pit. Oliver had dared me to jump, then bet me his Tamagotchi I wouldn't.

I might have been able to resist the dare—although it's iffy—but I really wanted that Tamagotchi. I'd asked for one last Christmas but had gotten a Barbie instead, which I'd given to my little sister Frannie almost immediately. (I did give her one fabulous night with Ken first. My Barbies were into sex.)

"You're really gonna give me your Tamagotchi?" I asked. I'd known Oliver practically since birth, and if I knew one thing about him, it was that he could not be trusted. All of his ideas got us into trouble.

He rolled his eyes. "I said I would, didn't I? And you're not going to break your leg. It's like ten feet or something. You can't break a leg from this height."

I bit my lip and looked down again. It seemed like more than ten feet. Could I land softly enough not to hurt myself?

"And you're going to jump too?" I asked, my voice full of suspicion.

"If you jump, I jump."

I nodded, working up that last bit of necessary courage.

"Move over. I'll go first," Oliver said, scooting to the edge.

"No!" I gave him a shove that nearly sent him rolling down the sloped roof. He was always showing off. We were the same age, but he was bigger, stronger, and faster—and he was *such* a jerk about it sometimes.

I called his mom and dad Aunt Nell and Uncle Soapy (more on that later), but we weren't really cousins. We were just thrown together a lot because our mothers had been best friends forever. They'd been pregnant with us at the same time and had given birth only two days apart. Oliver was older, of course, and you'd have thought those two days made *all* the difference. Half the time I couldn't stand him—the other half the time, I found myself doing everything I could to impress him.

I did not understand myself sometimes.

"So do it already." He checked his watch. Oliver Ford Pemberton *always* wore a watch. "I don't have all day."

"Fine." I moved a little closer to the edge and dangled my legs off. "On the count of three."

"One." Oliver sounded smug and slightly bored, as if he knew I wouldn't do it.

"Two," I ventured hesitantly, hoping I wasn't going to vomit.

"Three." He paused. "I knew you wouldn't—oh shit!"

I'd jumped. And landed badly, with a noise that can only be described as a sickening crack and a leg twisted at an unnatural angle beneath me. Before I could even register the pain and start to scream, Oliver jumped too.

THUD.

He wound up right next to me in the mud, landing even less gracefully than I had, practically head first.

He moaned as I started to shriek. It didn't take long for our parents to come running.

Turns out, Oliver had lied about several things. He'd never jumped off a roof before. He didn't even own a Tamagotchi. And actually, you *can* break a leg from a twelve-foot jump.

You can also break a clavicle, which served him right as far as I was concerned.

I ended up needing surgery, which left a scar on my right leg, and every time I saw it, I got mad at him all over again. At myself too.

I wish I could say it was the last dare I ever took from him, the last bet I ever made with him, the last time I ever *trusted* fucking Oliver Ford Pemberton.

But it wasn't.

Not even close.

Two

Chloe

NOW

"You can't be serious." I stared across the dinner table at my dad, who'd just ruined my life with a single sentence. "You expect me to work for *Oliver*?"

"It's only for six months." My dad shrugged and reached for a slice of bread, like it was no big deal that I'd have to take orders from that asshole for half a year. "He seems to think that will be plenty of time to train you."

"Six months!" I grabbed my wine glass and held on tight.

"It makes sense, Chloe. You want to open a distillery. He already runs one. And it's done very well over the last few years."

I knew all about his damn distillery—it had been *my* idea.

"Oliver is like family," my mother said. "You've known him since you were born."

"That's not *my* fault." I took a gulp of rosé.

"I think Oliver's nice," said my younger sister, Frannie, perennial sweetheart.

I shot her a dagger-eyed look. "You don't know him like I do."

"Who's Oliver again?" asked Frannie's boyfriend Mack. Actually, they'd just gotten engaged, so he was now her fiancé. He worked as CFO at Cloverleigh Farms, which was our family's business and encompassed not only a farm but a winery, an inn, and a wedding venue. I was kind of surprised he didn't know about this deal my dad had struck. He'd been in on several meetings I'd had with my dad about starting a small batch distillery here, meetings that always ended in disappointment for me.

No matter how much I argued that a distillery would be a great addition to our overall business and give us a modern edge, the fact remained—the money wasn't there.

"Oliver is my best friend's son," my mother said to Mack with fondness in her voice. "And he's so charming."

"So was Ted Bundy," I reminded her.

"Smart, handsome, successful." My mother went on as if I hadn't spoken. "He's really made something of himself."

"Which isn't that hard to do when your last name is Pemberton," I muttered, stabbing a grilled spear of asparagus with my fork.

"Pemberton like the soap company?" Mack asked.

"Exactly." I pointed the spear at Mack. "And his middle name is Ford. How hard can it be to find success when you come from not one, but two, massive family fortunes?"

"Now Chloe," my mother admonished. "Nell said he used his own money to start the distillery."

I snorted. "His own money. Right."

"Much the way you used *your* own money for your

college education," my dad pointed out, a rueful grin on his face. "Family money is family money. Ours just happens to be Sawyer money, not Pemberton money. It doesn't go quite as far." He laughed at his own joke.

"That's different," I argued. "Yes, you paid for my undergrad, but I paid for grad school, didn't I? I took out loans like a normal person does, and worked while I went to school so I could start paying them back. I'm *still* paying them back!"

"And we're very proud of you," my dad said, sipping his rosé. "But that's another reason why partnering with Oliver is a good idea. You know I wish we had all the extra cash you'll need to open a distillery here, but we don't. Not if you want to do it right. Mack can attest to that."

Mack looked guilty. "Sorry, Chloe. I can't argue there—if your heart is set on that expensive copper equipment and you really want to do this sooner rather than later, I think an experienced partner is a good idea."

I didn't want any damn partner—I was fiercely independent and wanted to do it on my own, proving to everyone that I could. But I was running out of patience, which had never been one of my virtues.

I set my wine down. "Okay, fine. An experienced partner might be a good idea. But why does it have to be Oliver?"

"Oliver is a natural choice," my dad said. "He and I spoke about your ideas a bit when Mom and I were visiting Nell and Soapy last month in Harbor Springs. He happened to be there at the time. Then out of the blue, he called me yesterday. Said he'd given it some thought and had a proposal for me."

My jaw hung open. I didn't know what I was more miffed about—that my father had shared my ideas with Oliver in the first place without telling me, or that the two of them had made this deal behind my back, effectively hijacking my idea.

Typical men!

"What's the exact proposal?" I demanded stiffly, trying to keep my cool.

My dad finished chewing, swallowed, and took another sip of wine before he answered. "He'll teach you what you need to know about the business, and when he's confident you're ready, he'll go ahead with the partnership and get you started up here. And he'll put up half the money."

"That gives him all the power," I bristled.

"Not at all." He leaned back in his chair. "Look, if you aren't interested, you don't have to do it, but then there will be no distillery at Cloverleigh. I promised your mother I'd slow down, think about retiring. She's got travel booked for us already this fall, as soon as tourist season slows down. I can't take on a project of this magnitude at this point in my life, personally or financially."

"The doctor said he needs less stress," my mother put in, patting his shoulder. "More time off. We talked it over last night, and we think this is brilliant. Oliver's offer is very generous. Would you have preferred we turn it down?"

"No," I admitted, crossing my arms over my chest. "I just wish you'd have talked to me before telling him I'd do it."

"You've wanted this for years, Dimples," my dad reminded me, using his old pet name for me. "Why be stubborn about this? It's the perfect solution. Right, Mack?"

"Uh." Mack went a little pale at the thought of having to weigh in on a family argument.

"Oh, go ahead, Mack," I said crossly. "You might as well weigh in. You're family now, and I trust you'll tell me the truth."

Mack cleared his throat. "Well, while I'm not privy to the details of the deal or partnership your dad is talking about, and I don't know anything about Oliver or his business, I can tell you that partnering up with someone who has the knowledge and means to see something like this through is a better idea than borrowing or crowdsourcing tons of money and going in blind."

"Exactly." My father nodded at Mack. "I spoke with Henry DeSantis about this as well, and he agrees. He doesn't have any background in distilling spirits, plus he's got his hands full with the vineyard this season."

"You already talked to Henry about this?" Henry DeSantis was the winemaker at Cloverleigh, and I worked with him a lot since I was in charge of marketing and PR for our wines and also managed the tasting rooms both here and downtown. He was a great guy and we were pretty good friends, which was why this felt like a betrayal on so many sides. I felt like they were all part of some Boys Club I wasn't allowed into but that got to decide my future.

"I had to," my father went on with a shrug. "After all, it will be Henry who's short-handed while you work with Oliver—if that's what you want, of course." He picked up his wine again. "I won't force you to agree to this."

Frowning, I stared at my fork and knife. Then I cut and ate a bite of grilled shrimp, mostly just to have something to do while I mulled things over. My therapist, Ken, had taught me the benefit of taking time before shooting my mouth off, even just two or three seconds. It wasn't always easy for me, but I was working on it.

"I think it's a good idea," said my older sister April, seated to my left. "Why not give the partnership with Oliver a chance?"

Why not? I had a hundred reasons, but here were the top two:

1. Oliver Ford Pemberton could not be trusted.

2. I could not be trusted around Oliver Ford Pemberton.

But I took my time chewing and swallowing. Another thing Ken had taught me was to be more empathetic, to put myself in another person's shoes. My dad was older, almost seventy, and his health was an issue. All of us—my mother, my four sisters, longtime employees like Mack and Henry—agreed that slowing down would be best for him. Deep down I was really hoping he'd turn over some of the general management of Cloverleigh to me … it only made sense.

I wasn't the oldest sibling—that was Sylvia—but she lived out in Santa Barbara with her husband and kids. I wasn't even the second oldest—that was April. She was the event planner here. She was awesome at her job, and I'd never heard a peep from her about wanting to do anything else. Weddings and other corporate events kept her busy, and she was always adapting to new trends. Next in line was Meg, but she lived in D.C., where she was busy climbing the political ladder and trying to make a difference, which had always been her dream.

That left Frannie and me. Frannie was the youngest at twenty-seven, but she'd recently stopped working reception at the inn to run her own little macarons enterprise out of a coffee shop in downtown Traverse City, which was about twenty minutes away. She was also newly engaged to a single dad who had three young girls and had just moved in with them. Between her new business, helping to raise three kids, and planning a wedding, there was no way she could take on more responsibility at Cloverleigh.

So promoting *me* made sense. I was fully dedicated to the family business. I was thirty-two. I was single and had no prospects or plans to be otherwise in the near future—my romantic history was a road pockmarked with impulsive behavior and regrettable decisions. I had terrible taste in men, and until Ken could explain to me why I always chose assholes over nice guys, I'd sworn off relationships.

But I understood that if I wanted to prove I was a team player, flexible and smart, a big-picture thinker and a cool-headed businesswoman, I had to be willing to make compromises and not let my emotions get the best of me.

I took a deep breath and another sip of wine.

"I like the *idea* of compromise," I began. "I'm just … concerned that Oliver and I might not be the best *fit* as partners."

To my left, I heard April snicker, which she tried to hide by lifting her wine glass to her lips. No one at the table knew my *full* history with Oliver Ford Pemberton, but April knew enough to recognize the awkwardness of the situation. I kicked her lightly in the ankle before going on.

"Why not?" my mother asked. "You two were thick as thieves once upon a time."

"Because I'm a hard worker, and he's a globe-trotting, yacht-cavorting, devil-may-care, rich, egotistical playboy. That's why."

"Now, Chloe. People change. Oliver may have been a bit *unruly* in his twenties but he's really settled down over the last few years."

"We don't get along, Mom."

"Oh, posh." My mother dismissed that idea with a wave of her hand. "You two may have scrapped a bit when you were younger, but that was just because you were so alike—so headstrong and competitive. But you've known each other forever. For heaven's sake, he even took you to his prom."

I gave her a flat stare. "His mother made him ask me. And you made me say yes."

"And you were *darling* together." She sighed sadly. "Nell and I always thought you'd be perfect for each other. It's too bad you two never—well, anyway, you're both so much more mature now."

I squirmed a bit in my chair. "I suppose, but I still haven't forgotten the mean things he did to me when we were younger."

"Like when he convinced you that you had Dutch elm disease?" April teased.

"That wasn't funny," I snapped, although the rest of the table burst out laughing.

"I never knew that," said Frannie. "How did he do it?"

"He told her that freckles on the nose were a sure sign, and if she started to grow hair on her legs, she should definitely cover them with peanut butter," blurted April, that traitor. "He told her that was the only known cure."

"Oh, that's right." My mother wiped tears from her eyes as she gasped with laughter. "I'd forgotten about that. I found her in the pantry one day just *covered* with Skippy."

"We called her Skippy for months after that," wheezed April.

"All I knew was that she broke her leg after he dared her to jump off the barn roof," said Frannie, giggling. "And didn't he break his collarbone jumping after her?"

My mother sucked in her breath, laying a hand on her chest. "Yes! Good Lord, I thought I'd had a heart attack when I saw the two of them lying there."

"It was more than a dare, it was a bet—which *I* won, and *he* never settled," I said, grouchy at the memory, "because he was a liar and a cheat and deep down he probably hasn't changed, and that's why I don't want to be his partner."

"This is making me feel better about what my kids do to one another," said Mack, grinning as he picked up his beer bottle.

"I bet your girls never put a rubber snake under someone's covers when they were a guest at the family cottage," I huffed. "Then hid under the bed to see how loud they'd scream."

Mack paused with his beer halfway to his mouth and shook his head. "Can't say that they've done that, but it sounds kind of like something I would have done to my sister."

"I find that hard to believe," I said with a sniff, "because unlike Oliver Pemberton, *you* are a gentleman. And you have manners."

"Oh, Chloe, for goodness sake," my mother scolded. "Oliver has manners. You two used to butt heads just because you were so close."

"That's not all they used to butt," April mumbled under her breath.

I gave her another kick in the ankle—harder this time—and tried again to be cool and rational. "Look. I'm willing to be open-minded about this, but I want to be honest, too. I don't know how well he and I will work together."

"He seems to think you'll work beautifully together," said my dad.

I rolled my eyes. "No, he seems to think it will be great to boss me around for six months. That's what will be beautiful to him. He'll probably make me scrub the toilets and mop the floors."

"That's not at all what he said," my mother assured me, reaching over to pat my hand. "He said he was reluctant at first too, since the two of you'd had some friction in the past."

Friction?

That was one way to put it.

"But then the more he thought about it," she went on, "he realized what a great opportunity it would be to work with someone as talented and passionate as you."

"He said that?" I asked doubtfully.

"He did. And he also said that he likes the idea of working with someone he knows he can trust, because he sees that as the most important thing in a partnership."

How ironic, I thought.

"I think you should do it, Chloe." Frannie smiled at me enthusiastically. "You're amazing at what you do here, but I know you've always wanted to challenge yourself to do more. I say go for it."

"How would this even work?" I wondered. "Would I have to move to Detroit for six months? What about my job here?"

"You and Oliver can work out the details of your schedule, but yes, I'd imagine it would involve going down there for some of the time," my father said. "As for your job here, your mother and Henry will work together to find a replacement."

I thought carefully for a moment. My gut told me this was my big chance—if I said no, I lost esteem in my parents' eyes and the opportunity to really make my mark here. I'd seem like the defiant teenager I used to be, or worse, like a stubborn toddler throwing a tantrum. But if I said yes too quickly, I'd seem too eager and the Boys Club would think they could steamroll me forever. I wasn't going to be their little rag doll.

Sitting up taller, I tucked my hair behind my ears and spoke with confidence. "I'll consider the offer after I hear for myself what Oliver has to say. I'll reach out tomorrow and set up a meeting."

"Oh, that won't be necessary," my dad said, reaching for another slice of bread. "He's already on his way up here. He'll arrive about nine, I think, and he's staying here for the night. If you're too tired to stay and chat with him, you can meet with us tomorrow in my office at eight."

My jaw dropped, and I felt the steamroller move over me, hot and heavy, leaving me crushed.

It wasn't the first time Oliver had left me feeling that way.

And it wouldn't be the last.

Three

Oliver

NOW

GOD, I WISH I COULD HAVE SEEN HER FACE.

Every time I thought about how mad Chloe must have been when her parents told her about the deal I'd proposed—and how they'd basically accepted on her behalf—I laughed out loud.

I hadn't spoken with her in a few years, but I could picture her perfectly, not only because I *occasionally* stalked—I mean stumbled across—her photos on social media, but because we'd known each other since birth and I was familiar with every single one of her expressions.

Hot and angry because you'd distracted her and then eaten the cookie off her plate.

Stubborn and determined when you bet her she couldn't run as fast as you (I had no idea why she took those bets—I was way taller with much longer legs and beat her every fucking time).

Outraged and defiant when you called her a chicken for refusing to do something stupid you dared her to do (she did it every time).

Narrow-eyed and resentful when you both got caught doing something dumb and dangerous that had been *your* idea, even though she never tattled on you.

Flushed and breathless, her dark eyes half-shut, her mouth open as you slid inside her, her hands clutching you desperately, your name a plea on her lips ...

Fuck.

Shifting in my seat, I focused on the highway again.

It had been a pretty easy Sunday evening trip. Most people were heading south on I-75, returning home after a vacation up north. My family had a summer place in Harbor Springs, but it was about a two-hour drive from Cloverleigh, so instead of staying there, I'd decided to take the Sawyers up on the offer to stay in one of the guest bedrooms at their house.

Had they told her I was coming yet? I started to smile again. Uncle John had said the family would have Sunday dinner at seven, and that's when he'd mention my offer. He'd invited me to join them, but I figured it would be better if she heard about the deal when I wasn't in the room. Probably she'd have turned it down right then and there just to spite me, and that wouldn't have done either one of us any good.

Despite what she was bound to think, I was doing this for both of us. I knew how badly she wanted a distillery, and I could make it happen—but I would need her help.

How furious was she? Would she even stay to talk to me? Or would she already have stormed out, furious and feeling like we'd ganged up on her?

Rubbing one finger beneath my lower lip, I figured the odds were about even. If she let her temper get the best of her, she'd probably left for home already, possibly after throwing something. If she took a moment to think reasonably about the deal, she'd realize it was in her best interest to stick around. Chloe's blood ran hot, and she was not my biggest fan at the moment, but she was no fool. And she wasn't terribly patient, either. If she thought I could get her what she wanted sooner than she could get it on her own, she might be inclined to play nice.

I decided the odds were probably tipped in favor of her staying long enough to greet me, sniff out the situation, and announce her unquestionable displeasure, if not her downright outrage.

But then she'd say yes. She never could resist me.

My grin grew even wider, and I pushed down a little harder on the accelerator, eager to get there.

Damn, I wished I could have seen her face.

Four

Chloe

NOW

MY FIRST INSTINCT, OF COURSE, WAS TO FLIP THE TABLE and storm out.

But did I? No. *No.*

Because I was not a tempestuous child anymore, but a calm, mature adult. A woman astute enough to recognize an opportunity and entertain its possibilities with an open mind. A woman secure enough in her own self-worth—mostly—to let bygones be bygones, forgive and forget.

Or at least that's how I wanted to appear.

To that end, after helping my mother with the dishes, I tried out some body language in my parents' first-floor bathroom, or what we called "the powder room" because it had a tiny adjacent area with a marble topped vanity and three-way mirrors that reached the ceiling.

I stood there for a full ten minutes auditioning different poses and expressions I might employ as Oliver made his pitch. I tried out detached, bemused, discerning, skeptical, cautiously optimistic, polite but pessimistic, and downright outraged. When I was confident with them, I quickly fluffed my hair with my fingers, applied a coat of an old lipstick I'd found in the drawer, which wasn't really my shade but was better than nothing, and pinched some color into my cheeks. I wished I was wearing something nicer than cut-off denim shorts, but at least I'd traded my white tank for a cute green blouse and my sneakers for sandals.

When I emerged, Frannie was standing in the hallway looking at me quizzically.

"Are you okay?" she asked. "You were in there forever."

"I'm fine."

She arched a brow. "What's with the lipstick? You weren't wearing it before."

"What? Yes, I was." I moved past her, feeling heat in my cheeks.

"Is that for Oliver?" she teased, following me into the living room.

"No. It's for confidence." I looked around, wondering whether I should be sitting or standing when he came in.

"This really has you worked up, doesn't it?"

"A little," I admitted, debating a casual pose over by the fireplace, perhaps holding a glass of wine in my hand. That's what I needed—a prop. "Hey, are you staying? Let's open another bottle of wine."

She shook her head. "I can't. The kids have a sitter, and we promised to be back before nine."

"I don't understand why you don't just bring them. Mom invites them every time. You guys could come more often if you did."

"I know." Frannie sighed. "It's Mack. He doesn't want to intrude on Mom and Dad's family dinner."

"Did I hear my name?" Mack appeared in the living

room doorway, keys in his hand.

"Yes. We want you to stop feeling like a guest in this house already." I went over to him and smacked his shoulder. "You're marrying in, you're family. And so are the kids, so you should bring them to Sunday dinner. Mom and Dad are dying to have kids around. They'd take the pressure off."

Mack smiled. "Maybe next time."

"Good. I'll see you tomorrow, Mack. Night, Frannie." I gave my sister a quick hug and Mack another slug on the shoulder before heading to the kitchen, where I pulled another bottle of rosé from the fridge. "Think I can open this?"

April, who was leaning against the counter checking her phone, looked over at me. "Of course. Good idea."

"Where are Mom and Dad?"

"Dad's in the den, and I think Mom went upstairs to make sure the guest room was ready for Oliver."

I uncorked the bottle. "Wish I had a rubber snake to put in the bed."

She laughed and set her phone aside. "So when was the last time you two spoke?"

I thought about it as I pulled a couple glasses down from the cupboard. "Two and a half years ago. The last time the Pembertons came here for the Christmas party. He brought his *fiancée*." I sneered at the word. "Remember her? The ice queen?"

April laughed. "Oh yeah. The blonde with the heels and pearls and designer handbag. She was pretty."

"Did you think she was pretty? I didn't." It was a lie. I'd thought she was beautiful—tall and elegant and refined. Cool and polished. All the things I wasn't. The sight of them together had infuriated me.

"I wonder what happened with her," April mused. "They weren't engaged for very long."

"She probably came to her senses. Here." I handed her a glass of rosé. "I'm going to watch out the window for his car."

She gave me a knowing grin. "Excited to see him?"

"*No.*" I snorted. "I just don't want to be ambushed. I want to be prepared."

"Prepared for what?"

"To stand up for myself! I don't want Dad and Oliver to think they can just call all the shots. And I feel like now that Dad's retiring, he's trying to bring Oliver in to babysit me. Keep me in line."

"And why would Oliver have an interest in babysitting you?"

I shrugged. "To torture me? Who knows? The guy's sadistic."

She rolled her eyes and lifted her glass to her lips. "I agree what he did to you in Chicago was shitty, but I don't think he's sadistic. And he must want to work with you. I mean, Oliver Pemberton isn't short on cash—if he wanted to open a distillery up here, he'd likely just do it."

"True," I admitted, standing a little taller. "I hope you're right. Because I really want this, April. I want to prove to Mom and Dad that I can envision something, do the research, lay the groundwork, and follow through."

"You can absolutely do it …" Her smile turned wry. "You just have to put up with Oliver Ford Pemberton first."

Three quick raps on the front door punctuated her statement.

We exchanged a look and took a drink of wine, mirroring each other since I'm a lefty and she's a righty.

"You ready?" she asked as I set down my glass.

"Yes. I'm going to stand up for myself. And I'm not going to let him charm me this time."

She grinned. "Good luck."

With my fingers wrapped around the front door handle, I paused for a breath. Closed my eyes for a second. Reminded myself that on the other side of the door was the same boy I'd known my entire life, and he wasn't any smarter or savvier or better than me. Just ten times richer, two days older, and five times as confident.

But I *knew* him. I could handle this.

Yanking the door open, I kept my facial expression neutral, if not cool.

And there he was.

Handsome as ever, the rotten bastard. Thick dark hair, cropped close above the ears and a little longer on top—the same preppy haircut he'd had since he was eight. It was a little tousled, but not messy like he hadn't brushed it, more like windblown in that I-just-got-off-my-sailboat-and-now-it's-time-for-a-G&T sort of way.

"Hey, Dimples." His blue eyes had the nerve to light up at the sight of me, his mouth hooking into that prep school smile.

"Hello." I was careful to remain expressionless, although his use of the nickname annoyed me.

He put one hand on my upper arm and pressed his lips briefly to the right of mine. "It's good to see you. Been a while."

Not long enough, I thought, but I bit my tongue. "It has. Come in."

I opened the door all the way and pressed back against it. He stepped across the threshold into the house, and I caught a whiff of him—a hint of expensive cologne, a trace of starch, and beneath it all, something boyish and familiar that was uniquely *him*. It made my nether regions tighten in a manner I did not like one bit.

Resisting the urge to plug my nose, I held my breath and closed the door.

Oliver carried a well-worn canvas bag over his shoulder, (monogrammed OPF, of course). I'd half-expected him to show up in khaki shorts and a Vineyard Vines T-shirt—which was his teenage wardrobe—but he wore jeans and a white golf shirt, which showed off his tan and his muscular forearms.

"Oliver!" My mother came hurrying down the stairs and embraced him. They kissed each other's cheek. "Look at you. So tall and handsome."

He gave her a winning smile. "Thanks, Aunt Daphne. You look great. Did you cut your hair?"

My mother fluffed her short, piecey bob. "I did. Thank you for noticing. Are you hungry, darling?"

"No thanks, I grabbed something on the way up."

"How about a drink? Cocktail? Glass of wine?"

"That sounds good." He looked at me over her shoulder. "Chloe? Will you join us?"

"Sure. I just opened a bottle of rosé. Is that okay, or would you prefer—"

"That's perfect," he said as April came into the hall, wine glass in hand. They greeted each other and moved into the living room, while I slipped down the hall to the kitchen. Taking a few deep breaths to steady my nerves, I placed the bottle of rosé and some glasses on the tray along with a small plate of crackers and cheese, and went back into the living room. My father was shaking Oliver's hand and clapping him on the back.

"Good to see you, son," he said jovially. My dad had always liked Oliver, and it was easy to see how much he liked having another guy in the house. "How was the drive up?"

"Easy," Oliver said, taking a seat on one end of the navy blue couch. "Thanks so much for inviting me."

I set the tray on the coffee table in front of him and poured him a glass. "Mom? Dad? Some wine?"

"None for me, thanks." My mother sat in one of the striped easy chairs across from the couch, and my father sat in the other one.

"Me neither," he said.

I poured a little more for myself as April seated herself on the other end of the couch, which left me no choice but to sit between her and Oliver. As I perched ramrod straight on the cushion, I gave her a dirty look and she smiled.

My parents inquired after Oliver's mom and dad, who spent a little over half the year in Florida and the warmer months at their place in Harbor Springs. They asked about his older brother Hughie's growing family, and his little sister Charlotte, who was expecting her first baby sometime this summer.

Oliver answered all of their questions politely and sent his family's best, encouraging us all to join all the Pembertons in Harbor Springs for the Fourth of July on Wednesday. "It's my grandmother's ninetieth birthday celebration too. We have plenty of room at the cottage, and my parents said to insist you come."

I rolled my eyes. They had plenty of room because it wasn't a *cottage*, it was a fucking compound, with a seven-bedroom Victorian house, a tennis court, swimming pool, and croquet lawn on the premises.

As he talked, I did my best to ignore him, breathing through my mouth so I didn't inadvertently catch his scent. Tuning out the deep, warm tones of his voice, which still surprised me to this day after hearing his boyish pipsqueak for almost half our lives. And I tried not to look at his hands, with their long, tanned fingers, which were particularly elegant and skilled. I knew this for a fact and wished I did not. He still wore a wristwatch, and I remembered one time when I'd watched him remove it and set it on a hotel nightstand.

Looking at it, I forgot to breathe.

"Oh, your mother is always on us to get up there for the Fourth," my mom said with a sigh. "She knows full well that's impossible until John retires." Then she gave my dad a pointed look over the rims of her glasses.

My dad held up his palms. "I'm trying, I'm trying. To that end, should we talk a little business, Oliver? I told Chloe about your offer to partner with her."

I took another small sip of wine and sat up a little taller. Cleared my throat and my head. "Yes, and I'm a little uncertain about the idea."

"Oh?" Oliver gave me an infuriating smile. "Why is that?"

"Because I don't trust you."

"For heaven's sake, Chloe, mind your manners," my mother scolded as Oliver burst out laughing.

"It's okay." He flashed the prep school smile at my mother. "Chloe has never pulled her punches. I like that."

"Good," I said. "Because some things don't change. Some *people* don't change."

He met my eyes and nodded slightly, and I knew he understood. If nothing else, Oliver and I had an almost extra-sensory ability to communicate.

"Maybe it will help if I explain a little," he said.

I gave him a fake smile. "Please do."

He set his glass on the table and looked at my parents. "When I started Brown Eyed Girl Spirits five years ago, the market was much less crowded. And I didn't have any grand business scheme—just a dream to handcraft something that tasted really fucking good." He paused. "Excuse my French."

"Your French is fine here," April said with a laugh.

Oliver grinned at her. "Thanks. Anyway, I didn't really know what I was doing, but I knew what I liked and I did my research."

"And it's gone well, hasn't it?" my mother prompted.

"In many ways, yes." Oliver rubbed the back of his neck. "The gin and vodka were well received, and while distribution is always a challenge for small producers like me, we manage to do decent business on site and we got into some local stores and popular Detroit cocktail bars. But the industry is getting more and more crowded—there are something like eighteen hundred craft distilleries in the U.S. now, and Michigan has more than sixty."

"Wow," April said. "I had no idea."

"Standing out is becoming increasingly difficult, and while overall growth potential is fantastic in the next five to ten years, in my mind it's just going to get harder for the little guys. We'll either be bought up by Big Booze, so to speak, or go under. I don't want to do either."

"And you think partnering with Chloe might help you stand out?" my father asked.

"I think a partnership with Cloverleigh would be a sound strategy," said Oliver. "The best opportunity for growth is within a small batch distiller's home state. I need to expand beyond the metro Detroit area, and you've got built-in tourism, the winery tasting rooms, a bar and restaurant ... it's all right here. Plus with Chloe's background in marketing, she'd be a great asset. Marketing makes all the difference—we need a good story." He put a hand on my leg for a second, and a tingle shot up my spine. "I know she wants to make a good whiskey, like I do. But that takes more time and investment."

"In the meantime, you're just looking for placement for your vodka and gin?" I asked, jerking my knee out of his reach.

"I do want expanded distribution, yes, but I'm also looking for a partner, Chloe. My facility in Detroit doesn't have all the space I need for additional stills or a barrelhouse, and as I mentioned, crafting a really interesting, flavorful rye is something I've got my heart set on. I've been experimenting a little, and I think I've got a winning mash bill. I bet anything you'll agree."

I didn't miss the word *bet*, or the twinkle in his eye when he said it, but I didn't take the bait.

"So to be clear," I said, "what you want is a partnership with *Cloverleigh*—the use of its retail space, distribution network, tasting room, some real estate on the bar's cocktail menu, and land on which to build another production facility and a barrelhouse."

He shrugged. "More or less. But I also—"

"Then why, exactly, do I have to work for you for six months?"

"I thought you wanted to branch into distilling spirits here. Brandies from local fruit to start?" He glanced at my dad. "That's what your business plan said. I have it in my bag if you'd like to check."

I glared at my father. "Dad! You *gave* him my business plan?"

"Hear him out, honey," my dad encouraged. "He liked your ideas.

"That's true," said Oliver. "I think your plan is solid, and I'm willing to invest. But if I'm going to be making a considerable contribution toward your business startup costs, purchasing stills and grains and bottling equipment and the like, it only makes sense to be reassured that you know what you're doing. Plus, I won't be on site up here all the time. I'll need you to oversee production in my absence, especially once we get started on the whiskey."

"It makes perfect sense," my father agreed. "All the research in the world can't compete with hands-on training. If you're serious about this, Dimples, you need to roll up your sleeves and put in the man hours."

"I'm willing to put in the work, Dad," I snapped. "No one can accuse me of being lazy."

"Chloe, dear, we didn't say that," my mother said.

"Frankly, I'm pretty sure I've done more *man hours,* whatever the hell that means, on the farm than Oliver here has ever done *anywhere*. And I've had the dream of handcrafting whiskey just as long as he has, I just didn't have his trust fund to get started." I stood up, realizing I needed to leave the room before I said something I'd really regret. "Forgive me if I don't jump at this opportunity to take orders from you, Oliver. But I need some time to think about this."

With that, I set my wine glass down and stormed out of the room, down the hall, and through the kitchen, throwing open the sliding glass door to the yard.

I needed some air.

Some space.

Some distance between me and those blue eyes. That smell. Those hands.

It had been years since they'd touched me, but I hadn't forgotten how it felt.

I hadn't forgotten anything.

Five

Oliver

THEN

"This is torture." Chloe spoke through her teeth, a smile plastered on her face.

"I know. Sorry." I did the same. Our mothers hovered with their digital cameras like vultures, taking photo after photo of us and of the rest of my friends and their dates fully decked out in formal prom attire.

Well, some of us were fully decked out in formal prom attire.

"Those shorts look so stupid," Chloe told me, struggling with the word *stupid* as she continued to smile. "Couldn't you guys afford suits?"

She was referring to the shorts my friends and I had chosen to wear with our dress shirts and navy blue blazers. My shorts were pale red, but all shades in the preppy rainbow were represented: kelly green, salmon pink, aqua blue, lemon yellow. Loafers, no socks. We wore bow ties, too. Mine was red and blue striped, and I thought I looked pretty badass, actually.

"This is a choice. Not a circumstance," I assured her when our mothers finally took a break to cry and hug and say things like *I can't believe this is how old we are.*

Chloe cocked a brow. "Really."

"Yeah. We don't want to be like every other guy who's ever gone to prom. We're proclaiming our individualism."

"In matching short pants. Got it."

"They're not *matching*; they're coordinated. And why should we be forced to wear tuxes or suits? We're graduating. We're sick of rules, and we're sticking it to the man."

Chloe rolled her eyes. "Jesus Christ, Oliver. Look around you. You guys *are* the man."

I glanced at my friends and had to admit everyone there was wealthy and privileged, headed for ivy-covered schools where we'd study business or law or politics or medicine, following in our fathers' footsteps, which would most likely lead us right back here to a big brick house near the water, where we'd live with our first wives and kids and dogs. We'd sail in the summer, ski in the winter, join country clubs, play golf on the weekends, and tennis after work. After a while, some of us would probably get divorced and move into a flat in the Park where our angry kids would be forced to spend time with us. Then maybe we'd get remarried and start the cycle all over again. It was kind of depressing, actually, how clearly I could see it all.

But Chloe was right. One thing we probably wouldn't be was powerless or poor. Was I supposed to feel bad about it?

"Hey, it's not my fault my family has money," I told her. "What do you want me to do?"

"I don't know, maybe use some of your millions to make a difference in the world? Do something meaningful?"

"We give plenty to charity."

"Like what?"

I had no idea, but I was sure my mother was on the board of at least three philanthropic organizations. I made some shit up. "The Shriners," I told her. "Those people with the funny hats that ring the bell outside grocery stores at Christmas."

Chloe snorted. "I think you've got your charity hats confused. The bell-ringing is for the Salvation Army."

"Oh. Well, I'm positive we give to both. And I'm donating my time to a sailing camp for underprivileged kids this summer."

"Are you?" She looked surprised. "That's cool."

"Yeah." I'd almost forgotten my mother had roped me into doing it. At first I'd complained because it meant getting up at the ass crack of dawn, and it would seriously cut into the time I planned to spend on my own boat this summer, working on my tan and trying to win back Caitlyn Becker. We'd been together all year until I'd fucked it up by messing around with a sophomore right before prom. Caitlyn found out and dumped my ass last week. *Maybe I should tell her about the sailing camp*, I thought. Chloe was looking at me kind of differently right now, as if she saw me in a new, more favorable light.

The last time we'd hung out, she'd gotten pissed about some comment I made about her stupid boyfriend, *Chuck*. I wasn't sorry, though. That guy was a fucking tool. I don't even recall exactly what I said, maybe something about him being the reason the gene pool needs a lifeguard, but she'd gone off on me, accused me of being a privileged, judgmental, prep school asshole. A sheep in a navy blazer and khaki pants.

Sometimes I worried she was right.

But I still thought I looked good.

She looked good tonight too. Like the rest of the girls, she had on a long strapless dress and wore sparkly things in her ears and around her neck. Her dark hair was done up, which made her look older and more sophisticated. It also meant her tattoo was visible across her upper back—that was something the other girls in the group definitely didn't have. It was a line from a book or something, but I forgot which one. She said her parents had been so furious with her for getting it without permission, they'd grounded her for a month. Taken away her keys, her phone, her freedom.

She'd also said it had been worth it. I dug that.

The moms were making the girls line up alone for a photo, and I watched them all smile for the camera. Their teeth were all really, really white but their dresses were all different colors. They sort of looked like a row of frozen yogurt flavors at TCBY. Chloe's would be key lime, I thought, but even *I* knew that probably wasn't something I should say out loud.

She was definitely the shortest girl in the group, but in my opinion, she was the hottest—another thing I wouldn't say out loud. She'd either take it the wrong way and think I *liked her* liked her, or she'd hit me. We were pretty damn close, but it didn't always feel like a choice. Even tonight had been set up by our mothers. And if her dark eyes and dimples sometimes drifted into my head while I was jerking off in the shower, it wasn't on purpose.

"So what happened with Chuck?" I asked her later as we swayed awkwardly on the dance floor, my hands on her hips, hers on my shoulders.

She shrugged. "We broke up."

"Good." Then I couldn't resist taking a jab. "Even you can do better than that douchebag."

She glared at me. "What happened with Caitlyn?"

"I cheated on her."

"With who?"

"Some random sophomore."

"Why?"

"I don't know." I tried to remember why I'd done it. "Caitlyn wasn't around one night and this girl was cute."

She shook her head. "You're a pig."

"Yeah, it was stupid," I admitted. "I actually want to get Caitlyn back. At least for the summer. I don't want to go away to college with a girlfriend."

"Do you love her?"

"I don't know. Maybe. I love the blowjobs she gives me."

Chloe thumped me on the chest and made a disgusted sound. "You are the actual *worst*. What am I even doing here?"

"Getting ungrounded." Her mother had shortened her punishment for the tattoo by two weeks after she'd agreed to be my date tonight.

"Oh yeah." She grimaced. "I guess I'll have to suffer through it."

But actually, we had a pretty good time. Unlike Caitlyn, Chloe didn't really care if I made an ass of myself doing the worm across the floor. She could talk to anyone, even the adults, and she laughed at all my jokes. It was comfortable and fun being with her, like old times. And she looked so fucking good in that dress. We'd never fooled around before, but I caught her looking at me once or twice, like she might be open to it. I couldn't decide how I felt about that.

After the dance was over, we went back to my friend Jeff's house for a pool party, and all of my buddies were drooling over Chloe's body in her skimpy white bikini. I stayed silent, although truth be told, I was drooling too. Since when had she gotten those curves? Had they been there inside that key lime dress all night long? I wondered what they'd feel like under my palms.

"Pemberton, you don't mind if I hit that, do you?" asked Lowell, his eyes on Chloe as she lowered herself into the hot tub with some other girls.

"Yeah, I do," I said, realizing that I minded way more than I thought I would, and not just because I thought Lowell was a dickhead. "So don't even fucking think about it."

The guys all gave me shit about my reaction, and Lowell started getting in my face a little, so I left them and went over to stretch out on a deck chair near the hot tub. I didn't want to get into a fight with my friends on prom night. And actually, I wanted to hang out with Chloe more than I wanted to be with them.

When she saw me sitting there alone in the dark, she got out, wrapped a towel around herself and dropped onto the chair next to me.

"Hey," she said over the music. "What's wrong?"

"Nothing."

"Nothing?" She lay back, crossing her bare legs at the ankle. "I don't believe you."

"My friends are being assholes."

"Ah." She glanced over toward the pool, where Lowell was busy flexing on the diving board. "That guy's a dipshit for sure."

"He thinks you're hot."

"Ew. Fuck him."

"He asked me if I'd mind if he hit on you," I told her, sensing an opportunity to be a bit of a hero. Maybe she'd be grateful enough to put her hand down my pants or something.

"What did you say?"

"I told him to stay away from you." Tucking my hands behind my head, I felt proud of myself.

Except then she got huffy. "Is that what you're doing over here by yourself? Guarding me? Because I don't need you to do that. I can take care of myself."

"Fine." So much for a gratitude handjob.

A moment later, she asked, "Just out of curiosity, what *would* you do? If he didn't stay away from me, I mean."

"Like if he tried something with you and you didn't want him to?"

"Yes."

"I'd fucking kick his ass."

"You'd get in a fight with your friend for me?" She sounded surprised.

"No, I'd kick his ass. There wouldn't be much of a fight." It wasn't true—Lowell was a big dude, and I'd likely endure a serious beating if I took a swing at him, but Chloe didn't need to know that.

"Oh. Well, … thanks." A few minutes went by. Over in the pool, girls were climbing on to guys' shoulders for a game of chicken, and in the hot tub, one couple had started making out. It was warm for early June, over seventy at almost midnight, and I felt kind of hot and sweaty, even though I wore only a bathing suit. I thought about Chloe up on my shoulders, her pussy against the back of my neck, her legs hooked around my torso, and my dick started to get hard.

Great.

What was I going to do if it didn't go away? Could I sneak off to the bathroom and take care of it myself? It didn't help that a soft breeze was coming from Chloe's direction and I swear to Christ it smelled like key lime pie.

"Oliver," she said.

"Yeah?"

"Do you ever think about me?"

I wondered how the hell to answer that question without getting punched in the face. Was she looking at my crotch? "Think about you how?"

"You know how."

I crossed my legs at the ankle and tried to keep cool. "Why are you asking me that?"

"Because I want to know."

I laughed. "I'm not sure you do."

"Is that a yes?"

"Yes," I admitted. "But it's not really my fault. I'm an eighteen-year-old guy and we don't think about much else."

"Girls think about sex too, you know."

"Oh yeah?"

"Yeah. A lot."

Hope, and my erection, rose higher. "So you've thought about *me* like that?"

She laughed. "Not even for a minute."

"Fuck off," I said, heat rushing to my face.

"Sorry. Just being honest. I've really never thought about having sex with you."

I said nothing because I was too busy being mad that she'd tricked me. I should have known better than to be honest with her.

"I'm still a virgin," she went on. "I'm saving myself for the perfect guy."

I snorted.

"But I *was* thinking about kissing you just now."

I looked over at her and found her head turned toward me. She was serious, as far as I could tell.

"Why now?" I asked.

"I don't know."

"Are you still thinking about it?"

Another nod.

"Then I dare you to come over here." I said it, but I didn't actually think she'd do it, so I was shocked when she got off her chair.

Moving over on mine so she could lie next to me, I thought my dick was going to bust out of my swimsuit. Was this for real?

Without saying anything, she stretched out alongside me, her head propped on one hand, the other still clutching that towel between her breasts. For the time being, I kept my hands locked behind my head—I didn't trust them.

"So?" she said after a moment.

"So what?"

"So I dare you to kiss me."

With my pulse hammering, I reached for the back of her head and pulled her lips to mine. They were soft and cotton-candy sweet. I kissed her lightly for maybe ten seconds and pulled back. "How was that?"

"Nice. Too nice."

"Too nice?"

"Well, Jesus, Oliver, if you're gonna take the dare to kiss me, do it like you mean it."

God, she drove me nuts. I didn't even know if she was flirting with me or insulting me, but if she wanted me to kiss her for real, I'd do it. I fisted my hand in her wet hair and brought her lips back to mine—this time, I opened my mouth and slanted my head, kissing her harder and deeper. I shoved my tongue in her mouth. I bit her bottom lip. I hauled her on top of me so her body covered mine. I knew she could feel how hard I was, but I didn't care—she'd asked for this. I kissed her until she could hardly breathe and she put a hand on my chest as she gasped for air.

"Oliver," she whispered. "We should stop."

"Why?"

"Because people can see."

"So?"

"So that's enough." She got off me and stood up.

"Wait a minute, that's it?" I braced myself on my elbows. "You dare me to kiss you and now you're leaving me here like this?"

She hoisted the towel up, rewrapping it around herself. "Pretty much. I'm ready to go whenever you are. I'm going to put dry clothes on."

Fuming, I watched her wander away, my hands clenching into fists. I knew I didn't really have the right to be angry with her, but I was. This was entrapment! Why'd she make me kiss her like that? Now I was going to be all blue-balled and tortured for the rest of the night, maybe even for the rest of the summer, if Caitlyn didn't take me back.

Girls. They were so fucking aggravating. *Especially* Chloe Sawyer.

I vowed I'd never take a dare like that from her again.

But I did.

Six

Chloe

THEN

"SHOW ME YOUR ROOM," I SAID.

"My room?" Oliver looked at me funny and leaned closer to my ear. The music at the bar was loud, and the crowd was noisy. "Why do you want to see my room? It's just a dorm room. It's a mess. And it probably smells."

"I don't care. I just want to see it. I'm bored." I glanced over my shoulder at Blair, my freshman roommate from Purdue, who was flirting shamelessly with Oliver's roommate from Miami Ohio. "It doesn't look like they're ready to leave yet."

"Yeah, I'm kinda bored too." He shrugged. "I guess we could."

"Cool. I'll tell her we'll be right back." Then I hesitated. Blair's sister was here somewhere—she was an upperclassman and we were staying at her apartment tonight—but I had no clue where she was. I didn't want to leave my roommate with a creep. "He's not gonna be a jerk, is he? I won't leave her alone with him if he is."

"Who, Beekman?" Oliver snorted. "Nah, he's harmless."

"Okay, give me one sec." I went over to Blair and whispered in her ear. "Hey. Oliver and I are taking off for a bit. We'll be back."

She held up one finger at Beekman and turned to whisper back, "Are you sure about this? I still think it's a dumb idea."

"Yes. I'm sure." I rolled my eyes at her doubtful expression. "Look, I just want to get it over with. It's my choice, so quit harassing me about it."

"Okay, okay," she said, giving me a hug. "But come back fast or I'll be worried. And be careful."

"I will." I made my way back to Oliver. "Okay, I'm ready."

Outside, the late autumn air was crisp as we walked down High Street from uptown Oxford toward the cluster of dorms on the edge of campus. On a Saturday night, the sidewalks were crowded with students heading out for a good time. We seemed to be the only ones walking in the opposite direction.

"This campus is pretty," I said.

"Yeah."

"Do you like your classes?"

He shrugged. "Yeah."

"Your roommate seems cool."

"Yeah."

It was like trying to talk to a brick wall, but that was okay—I hadn't come all this way for sparkling intellectual conversation. Well, technically, Blair and I'd come all this way to visit her sister, but I was also on a personal mission.

"You ever get back together with that girl?" I asked, pulling my hands inside my sweater.

"What girl?"

"The girl who dumped you right before prom. The one who gave the good blowjobs." It had only been five months since that night, but it felt like forever ago. Going away to college had made my former life seem as if someone else had lived it.

Oliver laughed. "Oh yeah. Caitlyn."

"Right. Caitlyn."

"No, we didn't get back together."

Good. A girlfriend would have been a complication. "How's your family?" I asked.

"They're good. Hughie got into Harvard's MBA program so my parents are all fucking geeked."

"Harvard, wow."

Oliver grumbled something I didn't hear.

"And how's your sister, Charlotte?"

"Fine. She came down with my parents to visit last month."

I'd pretty much exhausted all topics of conversation by the time we were climbing the stairs to Oliver's third floor dorm room. As we walked down the hall, which—as suggested—did smell pretty terrible, like a locker room and old, sweaty laundry—he did ask me one question. "You like Purdue?"

"Yeah. It's pretty cool. I ended up with a great roommate, so that helps."

"This is it." He stopped at a wooden door with a dry erase board on it, upon which was written EAT MY BALLS. He unlocked the door and pushed it open, gesturing for me to go in first.

It was a typical dorm room—two twin beds and two desks with utilitarian lamps attached to them were along the walls. One of the lamps was on. The window was straight ahead, shade down, and there was a closet on either side of the door. No rug on the wood floor. One navy blue comforter and one blue and white striped. Neither bed was made, and there were random baseball hats, sneakers, and sweatshirts tossed around. It was a stark contrast to my dorm room—Blair and I had matching paisley comforter sets for our twin beds, a coordinating rug, and decorative pillows, thanks to a shopping trip to Target we'd arranged beforehand. We kept it pretty neat.

"It's nice," I lied, taking a tentative sniff. "And it doesn't smell too bad." It smelled sort of good, actually—like the cologne Oliver had been wearing the night of the prom. The night we'd kissed on the lounge chair. I hadn't forgotten about that. In fact, I'd thought about it quite a bit since then. It was one of the reasons I was here.

Folding my arms across my chest, I moved farther into the room. I heard Oliver sigh and the door shut behind me.

"Which one's yours?" I asked, glancing at the beds before looking back at him.

"That one." He pointed to the striped comforter and I sat down at the foot of his bed. That's when I noticed the monogrammed sailboat sheets. *Of course.*

I bounced on his mattress a few times, trying to work up the nerve to say what I'd come here to say.

"So what do you want to do?" he asked, shoving his hands in his jeans pockets. "I'm kinda hungry. We could go—"

"I want to have sex," I announced, looking him right in the eye.

His jaw dropped. "What?"

"I want to have sex."

"With me?"

"Yes, with you. Why else would I be in here?"

"I have no fucking idea." He shook his head. "Ever since you texted and said you were coming here and you wanted to hang out, I thought it was weird."

"What's so weird about it? We're friends, aren't we?"

"Yeah, but ..." He struggled for words. "I didn't know *this* was what you meant. I haven't even heard from you since prom."

"I know." I lowered my head a little and peeked up at him through my lashes. "You still mad about that night?"

"Kind of." He crossed his muscular arms over his chest. He'd filled out a little since coming to college. "You fucking baited me into messing around with you, and then you took off."

"I didn't bait you. I dared you." I leaned back on my hands and swung my feet. "It's not my fault you couldn't resist."

A scowl appeared on his face. "Well, I'm not having sex with you."

"Why not?"

"Because it's a trap. You'll dare me to take my pants off or some shit, and I'll get all worked up, and then you'll decide at the last second that you don't really want to fuck me, you're just mad at your dad or something, and you'll—"

"Oliver, that's not what this is."

He eyeballed me warily and took a step back, dropping onto his roommate's bed directly across from me. "Then what is it?"

I took a breath and launched into the speech I had prepared. "I put off having sex when all my friends were doing it in high school because I wanted it to be right and meaningful, with the perfect guy. But now I think that's stupid."

"It was stupid then too."

I ignored that and went on. "The longer I put it off, the more it builds up in my mind. I want to get the first time out of the way so it doesn't feel like such a big deal."

"Are you drunk?" he asked, squinting at me.

"No! I haven't had a drop of alcohol tonight." I stood up and started pacing back and forth between the two beds. "Look, all my friends are being pressured into having sex with these total assholes who don't respect them and treat them like shit. I want my first time to be on *my* terms with someone I know and trust."

"You trust me?" He sounded surprised.

"Up to a point," I said carefully. "I mean, I'd never actually *date* you, but for my current purposes, you'll do."

"I'll *do*?" He stood up and puffed out his chest. "I'll have you know that there are a lot of girls dying to sleep with me. I don't need to be your *trust fuck* just to get laid."

"I know," I told him. "And I figure your experience will come in handy. That's another reason why I chose you."

I was leaving out the third reason, because I didn't want to say it out loud—that our kiss on prom night still had the power to turn me on whenever I thought about his body beneath mine, and the sensual way he kissed. I was attracted to Oliver without having a crush on him, which made him the perfect candidate to help me accomplish my goal.

He kept looking at me, like he wasn't sure whether this was a joke or a dream. "Why wouldn't you ever date me?"

"Because I've known you too long, and I know you too well. Your priority is a good time. You'd never be faithful to me. Plus you're immature, conceited, spoiled—"

"Okay, okay." He held up one hand and frowned. "I get the point."

"So you'll do it?"

"How come I feel like I'm supposed to lecture you about having more respect for your body?" he asked, shaking his head. "What the actual fuck is wrong with me right now?"

"I *do* have respect for my body." Because I felt like he might not agree to my plan, I decided to take it to the next level.

Step one—I grabbed the bottom of my sweater and whipped it over my head, letting it drop to the floor.

His Adam's apple bobbed as his eyes drifted down my chest. Beneath the sweater, I'd worn a very fitted black tank top with a scoop neck and a pushup bra. The look on his face was exactly what I'd been hoping for. Boys were so predictable.

Step two—I took off the tank top and let it fall from my fingers. "Come on. Say yes. Don't you want to?"

"Yes, I want to," he answered, his voice raw, his gaze on the rounded tops of my breasts above the top of that ridiculous bra. When I took it off, he was probably going to feel cheated.

"Good." Time for step three. I reached behind my back and unhooked the bra. But before it slipped from my shoulders, he slammed his eyes shut.

"Jesus, Chloe. What the fuck are you doing to me? I'm all …" He swallowed hard and squirmed before opening one eye and adjusting the crotch of his jeans. "Confused."

"Why?"

He looked at me seriously. "Because no-strings-attached sex with a hot girl is pretty much a guy's dream, and I'm sitting here trying to talk myself out of doing it. I feel like I'm in the fucking Twilight Zone."

"Look, Oliver. I want this. I've thought this through. I want to lose my virginity, and I want it to be with you." I started hooking my bra again. "But if you're not willing and able, I'll have to find—"

"Wait, wait, wait just a damn minute," he said, sticking his chest out again, hands on his hips. "I never said I wasn't willing. And I'm definitely fucking able."

I looked up at him. "Then I dare you to prove it."

"You're on." He reached for the bra, but I held it in place.

"There are just a few things we have to agree to first."

He groaned. "I *knew* it. What?"

"Number one—we use protection."

"Duh. Next."

"This is our secret. We never tell anyone it happened."

"Fine. Next."

"This is a one-time thing. Nothing changes between us. So no weird texts or phone calls or treating each other differently. We don't *like* each other afterward."

"I don't like you at all right now."

I smiled and let the bra fall. "Perfect."

His hands were on my breasts before I could even take a breath, and he pushed me back onto his bed so fast I felt like the wind had been knocked out of me.

Somehow—I'm not sure how, since he never seemed to take his hands off my body—he took off his navy blue henley and whatever he'd worn beneath it and stretched out above me with his bare chest on mine. It felt sort of warm and heavy in a nice way, but then the feeling was gone, replaced by a different one as his mouth traveled down my throat and chest and over each breast. My nipples stiffened and tingled, sending little bolts of arousal deep into my belly. Oliver wasn't the first guy to get this far with me, but he was definitely the most skilled. He did things with his lips and tongue that made me gasp and arch up off the bed. My hands moved of their own volition, threading into his dark hair. My fingers curled into fists.

I'd sort of expected him to get right down to business, so I was surprised that he seemed to want to take his time. As his mouth moved from one breast to the other and back again, like he couldn't decide which one was his favorite and had to keep tasting them both, one of his hands slipped between my thighs, and he rubbed me slowly but firmly on the outside of my jeans. This wasn't a new thing for me either, but it felt like it, because no one had ever touched me there while kissing me that way. The effect was dizzying and made my body feel loose-limbed and liquid. When he unbuttoned and unzipped my jeans, I was ready for it. I wanted more.

His slid his hand inside my underwear, but didn't rush to shove his finger inside me—he went slow, rubbing circles over my clit before stroking me soft and shallow, his tongue still teasing my nipple. He went so slow, in fact, I began to get impatient. This wasn't supposed to be romantic.

"Oliver," I whispered, using my hold on his hair to pull up his head. "Take my jeans off."

Without a word, he moved to the foot of his bed and yanked off my shoes and socks, my jeans and underwear. Before I could feel weird about being completely naked in front of him for the first time, he ditched the rest of his clothing and lay down beside me.

This time he kissed me for real, and I realized why that kiss on prom night had stayed with me. Oliver was a *great* kisser. He had a generous mouth with full, lush lips that commandeered a kiss the way a general commandeered his men. He braced himself on one arm and reached between my legs with the other hand. This time I did the same, a little hesitant at first, but discovering how hard he was, and hearing the groan at the back of his throat when I wrapped my hand around him, bolstered my confidence.

He slid one finger inside me as his tongue stroked mine. Then two. I moved my fist up and down the hot, rigid length of his dick, and soon he began to thrust in time to my rhythm. His breath came faster and faster. Pulling his fingers from my body, he rubbed the silky wetness over my clit with his fingertips. I wanted to move against his hand, but I was too self-conscious. This wasn't supposed to be about pleasure. I didn't need seduction.

He grew slick inside my palm. "Do you have something?" I whispered, my heart pumping hard.

"Yeah." Climbing over me, he got out of bed, went over to his dresser, and opened the top drawer.

I couldn't take my eyes off him—I'd never seen a guy fully naked walking around before. Oliver's body was lean and taut, with ridges on his abdomen, muscular shoulders, and hairy legs. His erection stuck out from his body, pointing diagonally up at the ceiling. I almost laughed out of sheer nervousness, but the next second he tore open the condom wrapper and began to roll it down his cock, and something about watching him do it stole my breath.

Then he was back.

"Are you still sure you want to do this?" he asked, stretching out over me.

I opened my legs wider, so he could wedge himself between my thighs. "Yes."

"Because now is the time if—"

"You know, Oliver, I really didn't imagine all this push-back. I sort of thought you'd just do it without talking."

"I'm not allowed to talk?"

"No. I just need an uncomplicated dick for this."

"Jesus." He reached between us and sort of aimed the tip of his erection between my legs, like he was about to shoot a rocket through a hoop. "This has to be the weirdest fucking thing I've ever done."

"Just do it," I said breathlessly. "Blair will worry if I'm not back at the bar soon."

He did it. Didn't take long, I have to say.

Not that I didn't enjoy it some. The truth was, it felt good being skin to skin with Oliver. His body was warm and strong, and he smelled salty and masculine. It didn't even hurt as much as I'd thought it would.

But I defiantly blocked myself off from any flutter of pleasure within me. I didn't want to enjoy this too much. The point of having sex with Oliver wasn't to satisfy my own desire. It was to satisfy my curiosity. Cross virginity off my list.

So I didn't move like my body wanted to, I held my tongue rather than echo the hot, abandoned sounds Oliver was making, I turned my head to the side when his lips came close to mine and told me he was going to come. For the next several seconds, his body went still, and I felt a faint pulsing inside me I refused to focus on.

Then it was done. Exactly as I'd planned.

Except … something wasn't right. We lay there afterward, Oliver's chest on mine, his breathing hard and fast, his lips grazing my temple. Then he dropped his head, burying his face in my neck. He kissed my throat. I swallowed hard.

I wasn't feeling as closed off from the experience as I'd hoped I would. I'd envisioned this being more like a business transaction, but my stomach was all knotted up. I was torn between wanting to tell Oliver that my rules were stupid and if he wanted to call me, he could, and sticking to the original plan.

"Chloe," he said quietly. "Maybe we could—"

"I can't breathe," I said, pushing on his chest. "Can I get up?"

"Oh ... sure." He got off me, and I quickly slipped out of bed.

Oliver and I dressed in silence, although I felt him looking at me like there was something he wanted to say. I didn't know what to hope for.

On the walk back to the bar, it was colder outside than it had been on the walk to the dorm.

"Want my jacket?" he asked me.

"No. I'm good." I wasn't good, I was freezing, but I never would have worn Oliver's jacket before we had sex, so I wouldn't wear it afterward. I didn't want him to think I expected anything more than I'd asked for. Instead, I pulled my hands inside my sweater sleeves.

He stuck his hands in his pockets. It was a few minutes before he spoke again. "So was it what you thought?"

"I guess."

"And you're ... okay?"

"I'm fine."

We walked in silence for a while. My mind was spinning with all kinds of thoughts, but I wasn't in the mood to talk. Truth be told, I was a little scared I'd say something I shouldn't. Something I'd regret. I had this weird pit in my stomach, as if I didn't want to say goodbye. As if I'd miss him. As if we were closer than we'd been before.

I had to stick to the rules, or I risked ending up with feelings for Oliver I did *not* want. I knew how he treated girls he dated, and I would never be one of those girls. He didn't respect them. He certainly didn't love them. He only cared about having a good time in the moment and moving on.

I never wanted to be the girl he left behind.

Seven

Chloe

NOW

OLIVER FOUND ME ON THE DECK ABOUT TWENTY minutes after I stormed out of the living room, lying in one of the chaise lounges and scowling up at the stars.

"This a private party?" he asked, dropping onto the chaise next to mine.

"Yes."

"Well, I'm crashing it." He stretched out on his back, folding his arms over his chest. "Beautiful out here. So peaceful."

"It *was*."

"Come on, Chloe. Can't we find a way to work together? Let bygones be bygones and all that?"

"I'm not sure."

He scratched his head and crossed his arms again. "Look. I can't change the past, but I can try to make it up to you. Let's put aside our differences and work together. Let me help you realize your dream. I know it would feel more satisfying to tell me to fuck off and do it on your own, but don't be stubborn, okay? Be smart."

I looked at him incredulously. "I *am* being smart, Oliver. My head is telling me not to forget all the stupid things you've conned me into doing in the past. My gut says you can't be trusted. My heart says—"

"What?" he interrupted, leaning toward me. He put a hand on my arm. "What does your heart say? Be honest."

I jerked my arm out of his reach and stared at him in the dark. "My heart is undecided."

"So let me convince you." Oliver's voice softened. "Give me a chance to show you why partnering up is the smartest, easiest, quickest way for us both to get what we want."

"And how's that going to work?" I asked. "By me coming down to Detroit to toil away in your distilleries with you calling all the shots?"

"Not at all." He paused. "Take a trip with me."

"What?" I squawked. "Are you nuts?"

"Maybe." He laughed. "But take a trip with me. There's something I really want you to see, and a story I need to tell you."

"What's the story?"

"First say you'll do it."

"Where's the trip to?"

"It's not far."

"You're not giving me much to go on."

"I know, but I promise it will make sense in the end if you just say yes in the beginning. Please, Chloe." He reached over and touched me again—my leg this time, the top of my thigh. "I want to do this together."

"You had your chance at that. You blew it."

"Don't you believe in second chances?"

He sounded sincere, and I let him leave his hand on my leg, but something was bothering me. "Why now? Why, all of a sudden, do you want to do this with me?"

"Because you're great at what you do. I know what you've accomplished here in terms of the marketing campaigns for Cloverleigh, from the wines to the inn to the wedding business. You're ambitious and creative and sharp, and I know you're a hard worker. And to be fair, it's not really all of a sudden. I'd have reached out sooner, but it felt more prudent to let some time go by, given the … circumstances."

The flattery wasn't lost on me, but I was silent for the moment, trying to do what Ken said and let things sink in before giving my answer. While I was ruminating, Oliver went on.

"I know I handled things badly in Chicago," he said quietly. He took his hand off my leg and laced his fingers between his knees. "I shouldn't have left that way."

"Never mind about that," I said stiffly. "I don't care anymore." It was a lie.

"I have no excuse other than—"

"I don't need to hear your excuse." That was for sure. The last thing on earth I wanted was to hear him confirm out loud what I'd known all these years—he'd been lying to me that entire weekend. That I had never been anything but a game for him. "The whole experience taught me some good lessons about trust. And you're right about one thing—it *would* be more satisfying to tell you to fuck off and make this dream happen on my own, but if I do that, it'll take that much longer."

"Does that mean you'll do it?"

"It means I'll consider it." I sat up and put my feet on the ground so that we faced each other. "You have one week to convince me. I'll go on whatever trip you have planned. I'll listen to your story. I'll give you the opportunity to sell me on this partnership and why it's worth my time and effort."

"That's all I'm asking."

"If you can manage to persuade me, I'm in. If not, no deal."

"Works for me." He held out his hand.

I hesitated, but eventually I put mine out too, and he enclosed it within his. His grasp was warm and strong, and the handshake was solid. It wasn't all business, though—a shiver swept across the back of my neck at his touch. *Damn him.*

"Thank you," he said. "You won't be sorry."

I wasn't so sure about that, but I let go of his palm and reclined in the chair once more. He did the same, and for a few minutes, we just lay there side by side, listening to the chatter of the katydids and staring up at the sky.

"This reminds me of prom night. Remember?" he asked.

Of course I remembered. "Yes."

"I never understood why, out of nowhere, you wanted me to kiss you."

I smiled secretly. "Good. I hope it's been torturing you for years."

"Tell me what you were thinking."

In truth, I'd wanted him to kiss me because he'd looked so handsome and broody lying there next to me. And I'd had a great time with him that night. But he didn't deserve that answer. "I was bored. You looked lonely."

"Bored? Lonely?"

He sounded so outraged, I laughed. "I suppose there was a fair amount of curiosity involved. You were always bragging about how girls were all over you. I guess I wanted to know what all the fuss was about."

"I see. And did that kiss satisfy your curiosity as to why I was such a stud?"

"Yes, actually." I looked at him again. "I thought you were a very good kisser."

"And yet you walked away."

I felt proud of my teenage self. "Yes. Because I didn't want it to go any further and I didn't trust you not to pressure me."

"Fuck off, I never would have pressured you like that."

"Maybe not," I allowed. "But I wasn't taking any chances."

"Well, you must have enjoyed it, since it wasn't long afterward you came to my dorm room looking for more." He sounded smug.

"That wasn't really about you. It was about me."

Now it was his turn to laugh. "Liar. You wanted me. You admitted it years later." He looked over at me. "Remember? At Hughie's graduation party?"

"Yes. I remember that night. Thank you for reminding me of yet another occasion on which you showed me why you can't be trusted." I swung my feet to the ground. "And with that, I bid you goodnight."

"Chloe, come on. I was just—"

"Goodnight, Oliver." Before he could say another word, I stood up and headed for the sliding door to the kitchen.

From there I fumbled through the darkened house, found my purse and keys on a table in the front hall, and slipped out the front door.

On the twenty-minute drive home, I felt so hot I had to roll down the window and let the cool wind blow through my hair.

For a minute, I let my mind wander back. To prom night. To his dorm room. To Hughie's graduation party. To that unbelievable weekend we'd spent together holed up in a Chicago hotel room seven years ago.

We'd had our ups and downs, but our chemistry was undeniable. We knew exactly how to light one another on fire in every way, good and bad. But that weekend—*that weekend*—had made me believe we were soul mates. I honestly thought we'd spend the rest of our lives together. I thought I'd been wrong about him.

So stupid.

Those memories had been buried deep inside me for years. But maybe it would be good if I dug them up and let them keep me company over the next week. Oliver had a way of getting under my skin.

I couldn't let him.

"Are you sure you'll be okay without me for a bit?" I asked Henry DeSantis the next morning at work. "My mom and April can cover inn-related business, but it's a really busy time for the winery." I felt terrible that I was taking off during our high season.

He looked up at me from behind his computer. "I'll be okay." Henry was rarely at his desk during the work day—he was usually out in the vineyard, pouring wine in the tasting room, giving tours of the winery to writers or buyers or sommeliers, maintaining his bottling lines, overseeing the fermentation process, or attending marketing meetings with me, Mack, my dad and various other family members. But this morning I'd caught him checking his email before he headed out. "Renee is going to come in this week," he added.

"Oh, is she? That's nice." Renee was Henry's wife. I didn't know her too well, but she was a talented graphic designer, and she'd done some work for us in the past. "At this point, I'll probably only be off for a week," I told him, "but things are a little up in the air for me at this point."

"That's what your dad said yesterday on the phone. Sounds like maybe the distillery might happen, huh? Your friend wants to partner up and invest?"

I grimaced. "Maybe. We'll see. First I need to survive a week with him to know if I can possibly take him as a partner."

Henry laughed. "You don't get along with him?"

"It's complicated. I'm going to try."

"Good luck."

"Thanks," I said, heading out of his office into the hall. "I'll need it."

Next, I stuck my head into my dad's office. "Got a sec?"

"For one of my girls, always." He smiled. "So you and Oliver are headed out today, I hear?"

"Yes, although I have no idea where. I told him he has one week to sell me on this partnership idea."

"That's what he told me this morning at breakfast." He nodded. "I think it's smart. Hear him out, get all the facts and figures. He didn't go into much of that with me."

"I will. I've got plenty of questions to ask." In fact, I'd started a list last night. "I want to know exactly how he sees this working with us *co-owning* the venture. I don't want to be just his silent partner. I want a say in things."

"Good for you, honey. Just remember, he's got more experience than you do."

My hands balled into fists. "Yes, I know, Dad. I'm not sure if we're heading to Detroit or what, but I'll keep in touch with you."

"Sounds good. Have fun."

After that, I headed up to the inn's reception desk, where my mother was on duty.

"There you are," she said brightly. "Oliver was looking for you."

"It's barely eight A.M!"

"I think he wanted to get an early start today." She smiled approvingly. "He's always been so ambitious."

I was dying to roll my eyes, but I managed to refrain. I didn't want anyone to accuse me of going into this with a bad attitude. "I spoke with Henry just now and he says he'll be fine without me this week. Apparently, Renee is going to come in and help out."

My mother's smile disappeared, and lines creased her forehead. "Is she? The poor thing."

"What's wrong?"

She sighed. "You can't say anything about this, but I ran into her last week in town, and when I asked how she was, she burst into tears. Turns out they've been struggling with fertility treatments. She confided that their latest round of IVF failed."

"Oh. That's too bad."

"She was so upset. Reminded me of when Sylvia was trying to get pregnant."

My eyes widened. "Really? I didn't know Sylvia had IVF."

"She didn't talk about it much. You know how private she is." She sighed. "But it was very hard on her. Anyway, it just goes to show you that you shouldn't wait forever to start trying to have children," my mom scolded. "You never know what kinds of issues you might—"

"Bye, Mom." I left her mid-sentence, unwilling to hear another lecture about putting off marriage and family. I had no idea if that was in the cards for me and didn't feel any burning desire to make it happen. I had my hands full with professional goals.

Thank God Frannie had just gotten engaged to Mack—our mother could nag *her* about kids now.

From the inn's lobby, which was starting to get crowded with guests coming down from their rooms for breakfast, I headed for my parents' wing, which was the original farmhouse, although it had been expanded and remodeled many times over the last 100 years.

I let myself in the side door, which led directly into the kitchen, where I found Oliver leaning against the counter, drinking a cup of coffee, and looking at his phone. He was showered and dressed, and his hair was still a little damp, so it looked darker than it really was. His shorts made me laugh—they were red.

"Good morning," he said, looking up from the screen. "What's so funny?"

"Your shorts. They remind me of prom."

He grinned. "Oh, right. I forgot about that. What a bunch of douchebags we were."

"*Finally*, something we can agree on." I stuck a pod in the Keurig and grabbed a coffee cup. "So what's the scoop for today?"

"I figured we'd take a drive, so I can show you the place I want you to see."

"How long is the drive?" I asked, watching my cup fill.

"Not long at all. But I was thinking we could stay there for the night."

Suspicious, I peered at him over one shoulder. "Stay there for the night?"

"Sure." He drank his coffee, crossing his feet at the ankles.

"Like, in a hotel or something?"

He hesitated. "Or something."

Sighing, I pulled my cup from the machine and turned to face him. "I'm not sharing a room with you, Oliver."

"Okay."

"This isn't some kind of reunion for us."

"I get it."

"And if I don't want to stay wherever it is you're taking me, I'm not staying."

"Fair enough."

I took a tiny sip of the hot coffee and regarded him. He was being awfully agreeable, for him. He looked handsome and relaxed, like he didn't have a care in the world. His soft blue chambray shirt—tucked in, sleeves rolled up—had nary a wrinkle, and the close fit showed off his athletic build. Lean and muscular, but not beefy. For a brief moment, I pictured him naked, and my stomach tightened. I shoved the image from my head.

"What should I pack?" I asked.

"Nothing too fancy. Comfortable clothes are fine. You'll want a bathing suit. Sneakers. Jeans and a sweatshirt in case it gets cool."

"A bathing suit?" I cocked my head. "Where on earth are you taking me?"

"It's a secret," he teased, his eyes lighting up. "Just trust me."

"Says the boy responsible for my broken leg."

Oliver looked offended. "I didn't force you to jump off that roof. You took the bet. And I broke a bone too, you know."

"You didn't even have the thing you bet!"

"Okay, not one of my finer moments, I agree, but we had plenty of good times too. Remember when we were twelve and spied on Hughie and Sylvia making out on the front porch?"

I laughed. "Oh yeah. God, they were so mad."

"And how about the time we took my dad's Cadillac out for a spin?"

"Definitely worth the punishment," I said, gleeful at the memory.

"And my mom *still* doesn't know which one of us knocked over her grandmother's porcelain vase playing Ghostbusters tag in the house."

I sipped my coffee. "You're welcome."

His slow, devious smile took me back years. "Thanks. Now go home and pack your bag, then text me your address. I'll pick you up at ten."

"We're leaving that soon?"

"No time to waste, Dimples."

"Do you have to call me that?" I asked. It's not that I disliked the nickname so much, but it suggested a certain closeness between us I didn't want him to assume.

"Yes," he answered.

"Why?"

"Because I like the way it bothers you."

I glared at him and left the kitchen without saying goodbye.

On my way home, I called April and filled her in.

"Oh my God, I wonder where he's taking you!" she squealed.

"I have no idea. He says it's a secret."

"A secret trip? That's kind of fun."

"Maybe. But if I don't get in touch within two days, check the trunk of his car."

She laughed. "Deal."

Eight

Oliver

NOW

I KNOCKED ON THE FRONT DOOR OF CHLOE'S TRAVERSE CITY condo a few minutes after 10:00 A.M.

"Coming!" Her voice carried through the screens of her open windows. A moment later, she pulled open the door. "Hey. Come on in."

"Hey." I stepped inside and she closed the door behind me. Her place was long and narrow, with a living room at the front and kitchen/dining area at the back. Her furniture was neutral with very few frills or homey touches like pillows or blankets, or even art on the walls. But the wood floors were nice and the kitchen cabinets were bright white, and the stone counters looked shiny and uncluttered.

"I just need a few more minutes," she said, heading up a carpeted staircase to the left. "You know, it would really help if I knew where I was going. We'll only be gone one night, right?"

Out of her sight, I winced. "Yeah, about that …"

She appeared again at the bottom of the steps, hands on her hips. "About what?"

I did my best to play it cool. Everything depended on my being able to convince her to trust me. "Well, I had a couple different ideas. One was that when we're done with our business-related trip, we could head up to my family's place in Harbor Springs."

She eyeballed me. "Why?"

"For fun, Chloe. When's the last time you took a vacation?"

"I'm not sure."

"See? You're due for a break. It's not too far, the weather is supposed to be gorgeous all week. Hughie and Charlotte's families will be there too, celebrating Gran's ninetieth. I know she'd love for you to be there too."

To my surprise, she actually appeared to be considering it. "I do like your family's place."

"We can swim, take the boat out, go waterskiing, play croquet, some tennis, have drinks on the front porch ..."

"It sounds tempting."

"Doesn't it? Come on, you deserve it. Give yourself a few days off, come say hi to my family, and you'll go back to work refreshed and rested and ready to get started on our new venture."

She pinned me with a stare, arching one brow. "I haven't agreed to that venture yet."

"You will."

Heaving a sigh, she turned around and started up the stairs again. "Come up here. I need help packing."

"Happy to." I watched her ascend, finding it impossible to keep my eyes off her legs in those little shorts she had on. Her limbs weren't long by any means, but they were strong and smooth and I remembered them wrapped around me like it was yesterday. "I'm just going to grab something from my car. I'll come up in a sec."

"Okay. Just let yourself back in."

I went out the front door and popped open the back of my SUV. I had several things back there: the small overnight bag I'd used at Cloverleigh, a larger duffle bag for a few days in Harbor Springs, a large black backpack full of everything we'd need for the overnight hike I'd planned, and a medium-sized charcoal pack I'd bought for Chloe. With a quick prayer she'd agree to the hike, I grabbed the pack and headed back inside.

At the top of the stairs in her condo, there was a bathroom and two doors off a long hallway. The closest one was open and revealed what appeared to be a guest bedroom and office. It held a twin bed, a nightstand with a lamp, and a desk. I continued down the hall toward the second door, which was also open.

Chloe looked up at me from where she was staring at piles of folded clothing on her neatly made bed. "You can come in. It's fine."

I eased into the room and set the backpack on her bed.

She looked at it strangely. "What's that?"

"It's a backpack for hiking."

"I can see that." She met my eyes warily. "What's it doing on my bed?"

"Well, you'll need one for our overnight hike, and I wasn't sure you had one, so I picked it up for you, " I said, dropping into an easy chair in one corner of her room. "You're welcome."

She stared at me for a few more seconds. "Overnight hike?"

"You're gonna love it."

"An overnight hike … with *you*?"

I locked my fingers behind my head. "Obviously."

"Where are we going to sleep?"

"In a tent. I've already got it packed in my backpack, so you don't have to worry about the weight of it," I said, hoping to sound thoughtful and generous.

"*One* tent?"

"There's a sleeping pad and bag tucked into your pack already—hope you don't mind I picked them out for you, but they're top of the line, of course"—

"Of course."

—"and I have all the food and water we'll need as well. All you need are some clothes and a few other items."

For a second, she said nothing. Then she shook her head. "You're unbelievable."

"It's nothing, really. Just think of it all as an early birthday present." I smiled benevolently.

She grabbed a pile of clothing and shoved it back into a dresser drawer. "I'm not thanking you, Oliver. Because I'm not going on an overnight hike with you. So you can take the gifts back to the store."

"What do you mean, not going?"

"You heard me." She tossed another pile into a drawer.

"You have to go," I argued. "You said I had one week to convince you. You promised to listen. You said you'd take the trip with me."

"I didn't know it involved sleeping next to you in a tent!" she said hotly, slamming one drawer and opening another. "God, I can't believe I didn't see this coming."

"Hey. We had a deal. You *shook* on it." I rose to my feet in protest, like it was me who'd been duped. "Are you going back on your word?"

Facing me, she stuck her hands on her hips. "I shook on that deal under false pretenses. You should have told me up front what this involved. It was bad enough when I thought we'd have separate hotel rooms, but one tent?"

"Fine. Maybe I should have been more forthcoming with the details." I held up my palms. "Mea culpa. But I honestly didn't think it would be that big a deal. You like hiking. You like camping. I didn't want both of us to have to carry a tent—it seemed like a waste of weight and space in your pack. And the place we're going is so beautiful, I thought you'd enjoy spending the night there."

"That's not the issue and you know it. I told you this morning I wouldn't share a room with you, and you said okay. You lied."

"No, I didn't! It's not a room. It's a *tent*," I said, as if that made it better, not worse.

She shook her head. "You're despicable."

"I promise to behave."

"Ha! When have you ever done that?"

"I'm serious, Chloe." I moved closer to her. "I solemnly swear I will not lay one finger on you, I will not say or do anything suggestive, and I will zip myself up into my sleeping bag and stay on my side of the tent. You can sleep with a frying pan in your bag, and if I come near you, you can hit me over the head with it."

A smile made her lips twitch.

"Come on. Say yes. It'll be fun."

"What if I say yes now and change my mind? Is that an option or will I be stranded in the wilderness?"

"You will not be stranded. If you don't want to stay overnight, you don't have to. We'll get on the ferry and come home."

"Ferry?" She looked curious. "Is it an island?"

I grinned, feeling victory swell in my chest. "Just fill

your pack with lightweight clothing good for hot and cool weather. Layers are good. Hat and sunglasses. Sunscreen. I've got bug repellent, water purification tablets, and toilet paper."

She wrinkled her nose. "I have to share a roll of toilet paper with you? That might actually be worse than sharing a tent."

I laughed. "You'll survive. Pack a different bag with your things for the cottage and we'll keep it in my car."

"Okay. Will I need anything fancy?"

"Nah."

"But your mom likes people to dress for dinner."

I shrugged. "You can wear anything you like."

"Are you sure it's okay that you're bringing me to your family reunion?"

"I'm positive, but if it makes you feel better, I'll call my mom right now and let her know you're coming."

"Please do that. Thank you."

I headed for the door. "Just give me a shout when you're ready, and I'll help you carry everything to the car."

"Okay."

I went downstairs and pulled my phone from my pocket. But after giving it a moment's thought, I went outside to make the call.

Nine

Chloe

NOW

UNBELIEVABLE.

How had he done it? One moment I was putting my clothes back in my dresser, and the next I was pulling things out again, tucking them into a backpack so I could go on an overnight hike with Oliver Ford Pemberton.

Just the two of us!

Sleeping in a tent!

Alone!

Together!

It was just like him. He'd known perfectly well what he was up to last night, and he should have told me everything. Instead he'd waited until I had already shaken on the deal and promised to hear him out, *knowing* I wasn't someone who went back on my word. Then he fudged the truth about staying overnight together.

"Asshole," I muttered.

After everything he'd done, where did he get the nerve? I'd admire it, if I wasn't so irritated that he always seemed to get his way. As I stuck items into the bottom of the pack, starting with sweatpants and extra socks, I heard him go out the front door. A moment later I heard him speaking through my open bedroom windows.

"Hi, Mom." A pause. "It was fine, not much traffic at all."

Underwear. Sports bra. Soft T-shirt to sleep in.

"Everyone is good. Aunt Daphne said she'd love to come for the Fourth, but they're too busy at the inn." Silence. Laughter. "I know, I tried. But Chloe and I are definitely coming."

Pair of flip-flops. Bathing suit. Tank top. Hat.

"Yeah. I am too. But remember, you can't say anything about it. Not yet."

Huh? What was he talking about? Our partnership?

I went over to the window and peeked out. He stood on my front walk facing a shiny black SUV I figured was his.

"I know, Mom, but we just prefer it this way. At least for now. It took a lot for me to get back in her good graces. I don't want to blow it."

You're not back in my good graces! I felt like shouting. *Not after you just duped me into taking an overnight trip with you!*

Moving away from the window, I whipped off my shirt, exchanged my regular bra for a halter bikini top, then my underwear and denim shorts for my bikini bottom and some hiking shorts that were light-weight and easy to move in.

"Okay, thanks," Oliver said. "We'll see you tomorrow night. Love you too. Sure, I'll talk to Dad."

I threw on a sleeveless yoga top, tied a plaid button-down around my waist, and swapped my sandals for socks and hiking boots.

In my bathroom, I put my hair up and tied a bandanna around my head, knotting it at the top. I packed just the necessities in my backpack—toothbrush and paste, face wipes, sunscreen, eye drops, hand sanitizer. The rest of my makeup and toiletries were packed in my small suitcase, along with the clothing I'd want in Harbor Springs. I took Oliver at his word and went casual—shorts, tops, some tennis clothes, a cover-up, jeans, and a sweatshirt, but just in case, I threw in a pretty white sundress and dress sandals.

I took my backpack down first, setting it on the floor just as Oliver came in the door. "You're sure I don't need to pack snacks or anything? I have some things that might come in handy."

He shrugged. "Whatever you want."

From my pantry I pulled some homemade trail mix and poured it into a Ziploc bag, then added a few protein bars and some dried fruit. "Did you talk to your mom?"

"Yep. She's beyond thrilled. Can't wait to see you."

"I'm excited to see her too." I crouched down, sticking the Ziploc in my backpack. "It's been a long time. Maybe since that Christmas party at Cloverleigh your family came to a few years ago."

"Oh, right."

I looked up and smiled, unable to resist digging at him, although at the time, I hadn't found it amusing at all. "You brought your fiancée that night."

"Why don't I grab your other bag?" he asked, disappearing up the steps before I could answer.

Clearly, his broken engagement was not his favorite subject.

From the kitchen counter, I grabbed my phone, charger, sunglasses case, and keys. After sticking the glasses on my head, I wedged the other items into an outside pocket, and tried on the pack.

Oliver came down carrying my suitcase. "Looks good. How does it feel?"

"Pretty good. A little weighty, but I'll get used to it." I walked over to the kitchen, took a stainless steel water bottle down from a cupboard, and handed it to him. "Can you shove this in an outside pocket?"

He set my suitcase down and tucked the bottle into a side pocket. "Perfect fit."

I turned around to face him and held out my arms. "Well? How do I look?"

"Perfect," he said with a smile. "Ready to go?"

"Ready to go."

I had to admit I actually felt sort of excited and exhilarated tossing my backpack into the back of Oliver's SUV and hopping into the front seat. I didn't know exactly where we were headed, but it was a gorgeous summer day, I wasn't at work, and I really did love an adventure. I sometimes hiked with April or with friends, but it had been a long time since I'd done an overnight. I felt free and spontaneous and—yes, I'll confess—even a little bit grateful to Oliver for making me do this.

It wouldn't be so bad, would it? He still knew how to push my buttons, but he seemed more mature. More focused on his goals and not just on having a good time. Maybe he was right, and this partnership was going to be a good thing for both of us.

If I could learn to trust him.

As we drove west out of town on Highway 72, windows down, my arm out, warm air rushing over my skin, I tipped my head back and sang along with Stevie Wonder on satellite radio.

Oliver laughed. "I forgot how terrible your singing voice is."

I reached over and poked his shoulder. "As I recall, yours isn't any better."

"Nope, it is not." He glanced at me. "Know where we're going yet?"

"I have an idea." I bit my lip. "But only because you said island."

"What's your idea?"

"North or South Manitou?"

He grinned but kept his eyes on the road. "South. Have you been?"

"Not in years," I said, sitting up straighter in the passenger seat. "I remember once going with Sylvia and my dad because she was into photography and wanted to take pictures of the lighthouse. I must have been about thirteen then. We hiked the island, but Sylvia's not really a camper, so we didn't stay the night. We caught the last ferry home." I found myself even more excited. "I've always wanted to go back, and I never have. Seems silly, when you think about how close it is. I've hiked all over the map but haven't really explored my own state."

"Well, if all goes as planned today, we're going to explore the whole island, top to bottom and everything in between."

"Cool!" I clapped my hands. "I can't wait! But I have to ask what this trip has to do with business. I can't imagine what South Manitou Island has to do with distilling."

His grin grew wider. "That's where the story comes in."

"So tell me," I said.

"All in due time. For now, let's just relax and enjoy the ride."

I stuck my tongue out at him, but a minute later I

was perfectly happy again—eyes closed, wind in my hair, Motown on the radio, anticipation in my belly.

I was glad I'd come.

After grabbing a quick lunch in Leland, we purchased sandwiches to have for dinner and tucked them into our packs before heading to the Fishtown dock, where Oliver purchased park passes and a camping permit. Then we bought our tickets and boarded the Manitou Island Transit ferry.

I couldn't stop smiling.

Oliver and I sat up top, and it was so sunny I needed my hat to protect my face. I grabbed my sky blue Cloverleigh cap from my pack, stuck it on my head, and pulled my ponytail through the back. Oliver wore a cap too—it was navy and said CSYC on it, which I assumed was a yacht club he belonged to.

I also rubbed sunscreen onto my arms, legs, chest and face, but Oliver said he'd do it later. He was already tanned at this point in the summer.

"You sailing a lot?" I asked him.

"A fair amount. I'm a volunteer instructor at a sailing school." He pushed his tortoise Ray Bans up his nose.

"You volunteer?"

He shrugged. "It's part of a summer program for underprivileged kids. My mom roped me into doing it years ago, but I ended up enjoying it."

"Oh yeah, I vaguely remember you telling me about that. Do you still have your own boat?"

He shook his head. "I did for a while, but I sold it to a friend in Chicago a few years back. I sometimes sail to Mackinac with him."

The mention of Chicago jarred me a little, and I looked across the deep blue water of Lake Michigan for a minute, away from Oliver. Were we ever going to talk about what had happened there? Did I want to? Would there be any point? For years, I'd convinced myself I didn't need any closure where he was concerned. But maybe I was wrong.

The ferry captain's voice came over the loudspeaker, welcoming us on board, letting us know someone would be coming around to collect our tickets, and telling us the ride would take about an hour and a half.

"An hour and a half," I said, poking Oliver in the leg. "Plenty of time for you to tell me a story."

He exhaled as if I was a big pain in the ass. "Okay, fine. But you shouldn't be so impatient. That's not going to serve you well in the whiskey business, you know. Aging takes time. You can't rush things."

"Thank you, I *know*. I've done my research, too. Now tell me a story, and it better explain what I'm doing on this boat, headed for an island in the middle of Lake Michigan where I will be forced to share a tent with you tonight."

"It will."

"Good." I stretched out a little, crossing my legs at the ankles and my arms over my chest, tilting my face toward the sun. "Okay, start."

"The story starts one hundred years ago with a brave and determined young Russian named Jacob Feldmann. He'd grown up on his family's farm, but times were tough. Facing widespread poverty, religious persecution, and starvation, he decided to take his chances in a faraway land—America."

I smiled at his dramatic delivery. "Go on."

"Like so many of his countryman, Jacob sets out on foot, bound for a port city in the east so he can sail across the ocean and make a better life for himself. And tucked inside one of his pockets is the key to his version of the American dream."

"Magic beans?" I guessed.

"Something better. Magic seeds."

"What kind of seeds?"

"Rye," Oliver said emphatically. "But not just any rye – this was an unknown variety that had *only* been grown on his family's land in Russia for generations. It had a big, earthy flavor that brought bread—and whiskey—to life."

I sat up a little taller in my seat.

"Now, he only has a handful of seeds—less than a handful, actually—but Jacob is confident. He makes his way west from New York City to Michigan and plants it. He chooses the state because he believes the climate and soil are similar to Russia's."

"Fucking cold nine months of the year?"

Oliver pointed at me. "Right. And it works—Jacob's rye spreads beautifully to nearly a million acres. People start growing it in Pennsylvania and Ohio, and as promised, it makes a delicious, flavorful whiskey. Jacob prospers."

"I feel like something is about to go wrong."

He tapped my nose. "Bingo. Two things go wrong, actually. First, it turns out that Jacob Feldmann's Russian rye is a finicky little princess. It can't stand mixing. The moment foreign pollen is introduced, the rye starts to lose all its distinctive flavor characteristics."

I gasped. "No."

"Within ten years, only five percent of the crop was fit for sale. But Jacob didn't give up—he knew all he needed was to find a place where it would be possible to grow only pure Feldmann rye without any intruders. But while he's searching for the right spot, the Eighteenth Amendment passes, and the whiskey industry dies."

"Damn you, Prohibition." I shook my fist.

"This means lower demand, and lower demand means farmers need to find other crops to grow. Rye falls out of favor. Jacob can't find anyone in a suitably isolated environment willing to take a chance on growing his seed."

"There's a joke in there somewhere," I snicker.

Oliver nudged my leg with his. "Keep your mind out of the gutter, Sawyer."

"Sorry. Go on."

"Now right about this time, something fortuitous happens."

"What?"

"Jacob ..." Oliver paused dramatically. "Falls in love."

"Oooooh!" I clapped my hands and wiggled in my seat. "Who is she?"

"Her name is Rebecca Hofstadt, and she's the daughter of a South Manitou island woodsman, a German immigrant named George. She grew up on the island, but left after the eighth grade so she could attend high school on the mainland. Later, she becomes a schoolteacher and returns to the island to take charge of the one-room schoolhouse there."

"Interesting," I said. "So how do they meet?"

"One summer afternoon, Jacob sees Rebecca walking along the Fishtown docks in Leland. She came often during the warmer months to stock up on supplies you couldn't get on the island during the winter when the boats aren't running. Well, the story goes Jacob takes one look at the beautiful Rebecca and falls to his knees in the street. He's never seen such a heavenly creature in all his life. As he watches her make her way along the boards, he hears the voice of

God in his head saying, *Marry that girl, Jacob Feldmann. She is your destiny.*"

"So does he propose right there on the docks?"

"Of course he did. He'd just heard the voice of God. Wouldn't you?"

I laughed. "What did she say?"

"She said no, of course, but in the ensuing conversation, he did learn her name and where she lived. Now he's even *more* ecstatic because he's at the Fishtown docks that very day waiting for a boat to ferry him over to South Manitou Island, which is a self-contained, self-sustaining agricultural society. He thinks his rye would have a chance to grow purely there. All he needs is a farmer to try it, and he finds one."

"Let me guess—Rebecca's dear old dad."

"Exactly. Undeterred by her refusal of his offer of marriage, Jacob asks permission to accompany her back to the island and meet her father. She agrees."

Looking out over the water toward the island, I imagine Jacob and Rebecca on a ferry much like this one, heading for their future together. "So how does he convince George to grow the rye?"

"Well, George wasn't really a farmer. He'd been a sailor, which was how he wound up on South Manitou—steamer ships used to put in there to fuel up with wood for their boilers. Back in those days, the Manitou Passage was a critical spot in the journey for ships traveling on the Great Lakes. South Manitou had an important lifesaving station and lighthouse to help prevent the shipwrecks that were all too common in those days due to high traffic, unpredictable weather, and the underwater landscape."

I nodded, remembering some of this from being on the island with Sylvia and my dad. "I think there's still a shipwreck visible from the beach. Like sticking out of the water."

"There is. We'll see it today on our hike. So George decided lumbering sounded better than being a sailor, and he decided to stay on South Manitou and settle down on the booming little island. But when the ships started to burn coal, the lumber business there died. He turned to farming, mostly to keep his family fed."

"He had kids?"

Oliver nodded. "Rebecca was the oldest of five. Well, Jacob must have been a good salesman, because he convinces George to turn over twenty acres to Feldmann rye, *and* he persuades Rebecca to marry him. He moves onto the island, builds a cabin, and helps George with the planting."

"And does it grow?"

"It does. Turns out the island's light, sandy soil is perfect for rye. They're so successful, in fact, that they persuade the other six farmers on the island to grow nothing but Feldmann rye, as it came to be called. And to this very day, it's the only place in the country where it grows."

"Really?" I glanced at him in surprise.

"Mmhm." Oliver looked smug. "And no one has made whiskey from it in almost a century."

My insides were jumping. I saw where Oliver was going with this. "But we will," I said before I even stopped to think.

He nodded. "We will."

Overcome with excitement, my creative brain kicking into high gear, I grabbed his hand. "Oliver, this could be incredible! Do you realize what we have? I mean, not only the potential to make a really good whiskey, but something even better—something that would help us stand out in a crowded market. We have a *heritage rye*, made from seeds brought here a hundred years ago by a Russian immigrant! We have the American Dream in a bottle! We have marketing gold!"

He squeezed my hand. "We have a story."

I met his eyes. "We have a story."

Ten

Oliver

THEN

NORMALLY, I TRIED TO GET OUT OF GOING TO THE Cloverleigh Christmas party with my parents, but this year I gladly jumped in the car for the two-hour drive down from Harbor Springs.

It was the craziest thing—I couldn't think of another time I'd been this excited to see anybody, let alone Chloe Sawyer. We hadn't spoken in more than two months … since that unbelievable night in my dorm room.

Sometimes, when I thought about it—usually right before I jerked off—I wondered if the whole thing had been a dream. But then I'd remember watching her strip off her sweater. Then her shirt. I'd hear her explaining to me why she wanted me to fuck her but not call her. I'd remember the taste of her skin and the smell of her hair and the sound of her voice telling me to take her pants off.

I'd recall how good it felt to get inside her and know that I was her first, that she *wanted* me to be the first. Somehow it had felt like my first time too, even though it wasn't.

I remembered that feeling afterward, foreign and familiar at the same time, because it was *Chloe* I couldn't get enough of. I wanted more.

But she'd been fucking silent afterward. Had she enjoyed it? She'd had an orgasm, hadn't she? It was too hard to tell with girls sometimes. I got distracted and lost control so easily.

But I'd tried not to go too fast. I'd wanted her to enjoy it, even if she was only doing it to cross "lose virginity" off her list. In all honesty, I'd thought her plan was pretty fucking stupid and figured she was eventually going to regret it and blame me for everything, but I still hadn't been able to stop myself from doing it. Not only because I was eighteen and obsessed with sex, but because it was *her*. Chloe wasn't just hot, she did something to me. I had no idea why or what. But ever since she'd walked away from me on prom night, I'd been thinking about her. It drove me crazy that she didn't want me.

Every girl wanted me! Why didn't she?

So I'd done what she asked that night, and it had been fucking fantastic. So good I couldn't stop thinking about it for weeks afterward. Other girls would approach me and sometimes I messed around with them, but somehow they never compared to her. They were pretty but boring. They never challenged me. They never made me feel anything.

A hundred times I thought about calling her, but then I'd remember I had promised not to. I'd recall how distant she'd seemed on the walk back to town.

And I was a fucking gentleman—I'd *asked* if she was okay. She'd said she was fine, but I knew her—something was off. She was *never* that quiet. Maybe she regretted it already.

I hoped not. I didn't regret it. In fact, I was sort of hoping she might want to do it again. And maybe she'd let me fucking text her afterward. Maybe we could visit each other or something. Purdue wasn't that far from Miami Ohio.

The first thing I did after saying hello to Mr. and Mrs. Sawyer was seek her out. I saw her across the wide expanse of the lobby, standing near the tree. My stomach did something weird and jumpy as I started across the room. I raked a hand through my hair, hoping my shirt hadn't gotten too wrinkled in the car. I'd ironed it myself.

She was with a group of people I didn't recognize, and she looked hot as hell in a black dress and tall boots with heels. Her lips were bright red. Approaching her, my heart began to pound.

She caught sight of me, and for a moment, she looked nervous. Then she smiled. "Hey, Oliver."

"Hey." I gave her a hug, even though we normally didn't greet each other that way, holding her a little longer than necessary just so I could breathe in her perfume. "How are you?"

"Good." She released me and put a hand on the guy standing next to her, a beefy-looking blond guy with a thick neck and a shitty haircut. "This is my friend Dean. He came up from Purdue with me for a few days."

Fighting off a queasy feeling, I held out my hand. "Oliver Pemberton. Nice to meet you."

"Same." Dean shook my hand, although he didn't look too pleased about making my acquaintance.

Chloe introduced me to the rest of the group, but I forgot all names immediately. All I could focus on was the way she kept touching Dean's arm and smiling at him with those red lips, and how he put his hand at the small of her back. It was clear they were a couple.

I wanted to fucking punch him.

As soon as I could politely excuse myself, I did, going right over to the bar and asking for some Woodford Reserve, neat. The bartender asked me for my I.D., of course, and I brandished one of Hughie's old licenses. It was expired, but the guy either didn't notice or didn't care. I took my whiskey and grabbed a seat at the end of the bar, away from the crowd. After tossing it back in less than two minutes, I ordered another.

I was halfway through that one, enjoying a decent buzz, when Chloe walked into the bar and spotted me. "There you are," she said, coming to stand at my side. "You disappeared so fast, I thought something was wrong."

"Nothing's wrong." I barely looked at her.

She paused. "Okaaaaay. Well, why are you in here by yourself? Why don't you come hang out with us?"

"I'm fine."

"Are you mad about something?"

"What would I be mad about?"

"I don't know. You tell me."

I tipped up my glass. "So is that guy your boyfriend?"

"Dean?" She folded her arms over her chest. "Why?"

Finishing my drink, I signaled to the bartender for another. "Seems like kind of a tool."

"You don't even know him," she snapped.

I shrugged. I was being a dick, but I couldn't help it. "I don't need to know him. But I guess he's your type. He play a sport?"

"Football."

I'd been hoping she'd say tennis or soccer or lacrosse or field hockey—something I could beat him at. But I was shit at throwing a football, and I didn't like wearing all that fucking equipment. "Figures. He as dumb as he looks?"

"Why are you being such an asshole?"

Another shrug. "Just being myself."

"Fuck you, Oliver. I was actually looking forward to seeing you tonight."

The bartender delivered my whiskey, and I took a big sip. "Why?"

"Good question." She stood there for a moment, anger emanating from her in hot, pulsing waves. "Look at me."

Reluctantly, I turned my gaze in her direction.

"Is this about October?"

"What do you mean?"

Her eyes narrowed. "You know what I mean."

I pretended to be confused for a second. "Oh, that. I forgot all about that."

"What?"

I lifted my glass again. "I *said*, I forgot all about that."

"You're lying."

Our eyes locked in a silent battle. "Does Dean know about us?"

"No. And you better not say anything. You promised."

I laughed. "That's right. I did. Hey, why are we talking about this, anyway? Isn't that against the rules?"

"You are being *such* a jerk right now."

"Bet you're sorry you gave your virginity to me. You should have let Dean pop your cherry. He's probably a much nicer guy than I am."

"He is," she snapped. "And you know what? I wasn't sorry about you until tonight."

That made me even more furious—with myself—but I took it out on her. "Well, it was a stupid fucking idea. I can't even believe I did it."

Her jaw dropped. "You're saying you didn't want to?"

I shrugged. "Not really."

"So, what, you just took pity on me?"

"Pretty much."

Her eyes glittered, either with anger or tears, maybe both. "I really hate you right now, Oliver. Thanks for ruining my Christmas." She spun around and took off, her boot heels clacking angrily on the floor.

I felt like shit. My Christmas was ruined too, but it was my own damn fault. I'd built up seeing her again in my head too much. What the hell was I expecting? She'd made it clear from the start she didn't want me. That she would never want me, not like that. I wasn't good enough for Chloe Sawyer.

Well, fuck her. And fuck these feelings. I hadn't asked for them, and I didn't want them.

I wished I knew how to make them go away.

Eleven

Chloe

THEN

"Do we *have* to stay the night?" I asked my mom as we got out of the car in front of the Pembertons' place in Harbor Springs.

"For heaven's sake, Chloe, we just got here." She gave me a Mom Look that said *mind your manners*.

Sullen and pouting, I watched my dad hand his keys to the valet. "I was just asking."

"Well, Hughie is our godson, and graduating from Harvard with an M.B.A is a big deal. This party is important to him, to his parents, and to us."

"Fine." I followed her around to the back of the car, where another valet was pulling our overnight bags from the trunk. Since my three older sisters weren't living at home that summer, it was just my parents, Frannie, and me. "But I won't know anyone here, and it's going to be boring sitting around all day and night."

"Nonsense," my mother said, slinging her bag over her shoulder. "You know the entire family. And Oliver's home.

When's the last time you two saw each other?"

"I don't know," I muttered as we trudged up the wide front steps of the wraparound porch. It wasn't true—I knew exactly when it was: Cloverleigh's Christmas party our freshman year of college, when he'd implied that he'd only had sex with me out of pity and hadn't even enjoyed it. It was the most hurtful thing anyone had ever said to me. Even now, more than three years later, it still stung. I'd never forgive him, and I'd ignored the lame, apologetic texts he'd sent. I'd refused to visit his family's home or attend any function where I knew he'd be in attendance.

Even now, I didn't want to see him. The only thing that would make this day bearable was a stiff drink. Several stiff drinks.

"I'll hang out with you," Frannie offered as my mom knocked on the front door.

"Thanks." I gave her a half-hearted smile. Frannie was sweet, but at seventeen, she wasn't old enough to drink with me and wasn't the type to sneak it. We were nothing alike. It kind of made me feel worse.

We greeted Aunt Nell and Uncle Soapy with hugs in the foyer, and followed a uniformed housekeeper upstairs to our rooms. Frannie and I were sharing a bedroom, the same bedroom I'd been staying in when Oliver put the fucking rubber snake in my bed. It looked exactly the same as it had then. Two twin beds, white wicker nightstand between them, white wicker dresser, and floral *everything*—bedspreads, rug, curtains, sheets, pillows.

"Want to change into our suits?" Frannie asked. "Go swimming or something?"

"Nah." I took my sandals off and flopped back onto one of the beds. "I'm actually not feeling that well. Can you tell

Mom I have cramps and I'm resting?"

The look she gave me told me she knew I was lying, but she dutifully agreed to do what I asked. "Okay. I'm going down. Text me if you change your mind."

"I will. Can you shut the door on your way out? Thanks."

When she was gone, I crossed my feet at the ankles and closed my eyes. I'm not sure how long I lay there before I heard a knock.

Assuming it was Frannie, I didn't even open my eyes. "Come in."

The door creaked opened and shut. "Hey."

That was definitely not Frannie's voice. My eyes flew open and I sat up. Leaning back against the bedroom door was Oliver.

He looked *good.* My heart started to pound, traitorous thing. "What are you doing up here?"

"Looking for you."

"Why?"

"I don't know. Haven't seen you in a while. Your mom said to come find you."

Of *course* it hadn't been his idea to seek me out. I studied him for a moment, annoyed that he'd gotten even more handsome as he'd matured. That chiseled Pemberton jaw. The bronzed skin. The dark hair dusted with gold from the sun. Even from ten feet away, I could see how thick his lashes were, how perfectly they framed his bright blue eyes. Something stirred inside me.

No.

I lay back again and shut my eyes. He didn't give a shit about me. "Well, I don't want to be found. I don't even want to be here."

"I don't either." He paused. "You still mad at me?"

"Yes. So go away."

"Can't we talk about it?"

For a moment I was going to refuse to say anything more to him, but then I changed my mind. "Why? So you can insult me again?"

"What do you mean?"

"You were a real dick to me last time we talked."

"At the Christmas party?"

"Yes, at the Christmas party," I parroted.

"Chloe, that was like three years ago."

I opened my eyes and gave him a look I hoped would scorch his eyeballs.

"I said I was sorry. Didn't you get my texts?"

"Yes. I deleted them."

"Why?"

"Because you fucking hurt my feelings, Oliver." I paused, wanting to ask a question and yet dreading the answer. In the end, I couldn't resist. "Did you mean those things you said?"

"No."

"Then why'd you say them?"

"I don't know." He paused. "I think I was pissed you had a boyfriend."

"Why?"

"Because I was hoping you'd want to have sex with me again."

Wait … what? I sat up and looked at him. "You were?"

He shrugged. "Yes. So he was pretty inconvenient."

"I didn't think you cared."

"I didn't think *you* cared. Plus, he looked stupid."

I folded my arms over my chest. "You think all my boyfriends look stupid."

"That's because you have terrible taste in guys."

I frowned. "Didn't you come here to apologize? Because if you're hoping I'll finally accept, you might not want to insult me."

"Sorry. Will you accept?"

Exhaling, I lay down again. "I guess. Especially if you bring me a drink."

"What do you want?"

"I don't care. Something strong."

"Say no more."

I heard the door open and close again, and when I peeked, I was alone in the room. For a second, I thought about locking him out—it would serve him right—but a drink sounded good, and I felt a little better knowing that he hadn't meant the cruel things he'd said at the party. He'd been jealous was all.

Jealous!

That must mean that he *had* enjoyed himself that night in his dorm. What a liar. Why couldn't he have just been honest with me? It was always games with him. That was exactly the reason I'd forced myself not to reach out after that night in his dorm room, no matter how often I thought of him or wondered if he ever thought of me.

A few minutes later, he knocked again. Figuring he was carrying two drinks, I got up and opened the door.

"Thanks," he said, entering the room with two old fashioned glasses full of amber liquid. "Hope you like good scotch. I raided Soapy's best stuff."

"I might. I've never tried it."

"You're missing out. Here, take a sip. If you don't like it, I'll get you something else." He handed me one of the glasses.

I took it from him and sniffed. "Whoa. Smells strong."

"Taste it."

I wet my lips with the potent stuff and licked them. Considered. "I like it. Might take a little getting used to, but it's interesting. Kind of … smoky."

"I want to visit this distillery when I go to Scotland."

"You're going to Scotland?" I sat down on the bed again, and he sat across from me, on Frannie's bed.

"Well, I'm going to Europe with some friends for a couple months. We're going to backpack all around, but Scotland is definitely on my list. I'm really interested in the distilleries."

"Cool. When do you leave?"

"Day after tomorrow."

I nodded. Sipped again. "I hear you're heading to Boston for grad school?"

"Yeah. Tufts." He took a big swallow. "Not Harvard or anything."

"So what? Tufts is a great school. You should be proud."

"Tell that to Hughie. I swear to God, he thinks he shits gold just because he went to Harvard. I can't even listen to him talk. Or my parents, either. I mean, maybe I don't *want* to follow in my brother's footsteps, and my dad's footsteps, and my grandfather's footsteps. Did they ever think of that? Maybe it has nothing to do with getting into Harvard. Maybe I want to make my own path."

"*Did* you get into Harvard?"

"No," he admitted with a scowl. "But I wouldn't have gone there anyway."

Unsure how to respond, I tasted the scotch again. I liked the way the flavors in the scotch didn't come out right away—you had to let it linger on your tongue a little bit to discover them. I decided to change the subject. "Are you excited about your trip?"

"Yeah. I gotta get the fuck out of here." He took another drink. "What about you? What are you doing in the fall?"

"Heading for Chicago. I got a job with a marketing firm there, and I'm going to take some graduate classes too."

"Cool. I love Chicago."

"Then you'll have to come visit me," I told him, and I was surprised to find myself hoping he really would.

He smiled. "Maybe I will."

We talked for a while. It was nice to hang out again, just the two of us. He told me about the death of his grandfather, and how hard that had been on him because they'd been so close. "He didn't care that I hadn't gone to Harvard. He always told me to do my own thing."

I talked about feeling frustrated with my parents because they refused to believe that Cloverleigh's brand needed a serious overhaul, with a new website, more advertising, and a presence on social media. "They don't take me seriously at all," I complained. "They just want to keep doing things the way they've always done them, and it's a huge mistake."

"Why won't they listen to you? You got a degree in marketing, right?"

"Right." I tossed a hand in the air. "Who knows? Maybe they're upset I don't want to move back home right away and work for them. So far, none of their kids has really shown an interest in taking over—Sylvia got married and moved away, April is working in New York, Meg's at law school in D.C."

"Do you have any interest in working for Cloverleigh?" he asked.

"I do," I said hesitantly, "but I'd like to get out and live a little first, you know? I've spent my entire life on that farm, and I love it, but I want to experience other things."

"I get that. God knows I have no interest in the soap business."

I laughed. "What *do* you want to do?"

"I'm not sure yet," he said, swirling the last little bit of scotch left in his glass before tossing it back. "Mostly I just want to have fun. You want another drink?"

"Sure. Do you think we need to make an appearance at the party? It's almost six."

"Fuck the party. I'll be right back." He took my glass and headed out of the room, returning with two more generous pours a few minutes later.

I have no idea how much time passed, but by the time we finished our second drink, the sun had gone down, we'd switched on a lamp, and we were sitting on the floor between the two beds, laughing about the rubber snake incident.

"Someday I'm going to get you back for that," I told him, setting my empty glass on the nightstand. "You better lock your door tonight."

"I'd never lock you out."

Our eyes met, and my breath caught in my chest.

"So are we ever going to talk about it?" he asked.

"Talk about what?"

"That night in my room."

My face immediately felt flushed. "Why do we need to talk about it?"

"Because I have questions."

"What do you want to know?"

"For one thing, why me? For real."

"I told you. I needed someone I could trust." I hesitated, figuring I was just tipsy enough to admit the truth. "Also, I was attracted to you."

"Aha!" He looked smug. "I fucking knew it."

"Congratulations."

He was quiet for a moment. "Do you still regret it, like you said?"

I sighed. "I did, after you were so mean at the Christmas party. But now … I guess not. I mean, I don't like that it messed up our friendship for three years, but I suppose the event happened exactly like I wanted it to. And in the end, I'm glad it was you."

He smiled, and it sent something warm and tingly up my spine. "Good. So did you have sex with that guy Dean?"

I narrowed my eyes. Just when I felt affectionate toward him, he had to ruin it. "What does that have to do with anything?"

"I'm curious."

"Not that it's any of your business, but yes."

"Was he better than me?"

Rolling my eyes, I started to laugh. "Jesus Christ, Oliver. Are you going to ask me whose dick was bigger?"

"No." And then a second later he puffed up his chest. "Wait, was mine bigger? It was, wasn't it?"

That made me laugh even harder. He was so predictable. "Sorry," I wheezed. "I don't remember." It was a lie—Oliver's *had* been bigger. Maybe it was simply that he was my first, but in my memory, he was bigger than all three of the guys I'd been with since him. The best kisser too. By far.

"Did he make you come?" Oliver demanded, setting his empty glass on the nightstand. He was clearly worked up about this.

"Uh, no, he didn't." I paused. "But then, neither did you."

"I didn't?" He seemed genuinely surprised, which set me off again.

Shaking my head, I grabbed my stomach and giggled uncontrollably. "No. Sorry. Although, in your defense, I'm not sure you had time. It was over too quickly."

His jaw dropped, then he clenched it. "Give me another chance," he demanded. "Right now."

"What?" I stared at him, trying to catch my breath. "Are you crazy?"

"No. I'm totally serious, Chloe. You have to give me another chance."

"Why?"

"Because what if girls have been faking it with me? What if I have no idea what I'm doing? What if I'm a clueless, selfish asshole in bed? I need you to teach me."

"I'm sure you're fine." I got to my feet, feeling like I needed some air. "Let's go down to the party."

"Don't go!" He jumped up and grabbed my arm. "Listen, you'd be doing me a favor, just like I did you a favor. Then we'd be even."

I stared at him. "Are you drunk?"

"No. Are you?"

"No."

"Then let me give you an orgasm."

"You're out of your mind." I shook him off and went for the door, but he vaulted over Frannie's bed and blocked it.

"You're not leaving until I make you come."

His words were turning me on, but I couldn't give in. "Oliver, we just spent three years not talking because we had sex."

"Worth it."

I narrowed my eyes at him. "Get out of my way, asshole."

"No."

There was no chance of my out-muscling him. I thought about kicking him in the balls, but wasn't sure I could stoop so low. There had to be a way to outsmart him. Turning around, I ran over to my bag, which was on the floor at the foot of my bed, and reached inside to grab my phone. I'd text Frannie, and then—"Hey!"

Oliver had tried to swipe the phone from me, but I was quick enough to switch it to the other hand and keep it out of his reach.

"Knock it off!" I yelled as he struggled to get at it. I jumped up on my bed, bounced off Frannie's, and went running around the perimeter of the room.

He cut me off by the dresser and I shrieked as he made another grab at my phone, managing to duck beneath his arms and make a run for the door. But just as I closed my fingers around the handle and pulled, his hand shot out above me and slammed it shut.

"God, you are *such* a jerk!" I yanked on the handle but it was no use. He had me prisoner.

His front pressed up against my back. My cheek was on the door. Both of us were breathing hard. "You want this," he said. "Admit it. You wanted me then and you want me now."

"I want you to let me out of here, you arrogant son of a bitch," I seethed through clenched teeth. "I knew I shouldn't have trusted you."

"So scream." His voice was low in my ear, and then his mouth was on my neck. "Text your sister. Call for help. Call 911, for fuck's sake." One hand snuck around my waist and slid down the front of my dress. "I won't stop you."

I knew I should say no, but his tongue was doing things on my throat and his fingers were edging beneath the hem of my shift and wandering up my inner thighs. Then there was his voice, all deep and intense.

"But I don't think you really want to go. I think you want to see what it's like to be with me again." His fingertips rubbed me over my thin lace panties. "I'm much more patient now. And I've got all kinds of new tricks."

"You do?"

"Mmhm." He turned me around, putting my back against the door. His lips hovered above mine. "I bet I can make you come within five minutes." His expression was cocky. "Care to bet against me?"

I bit my tongue, refusing to reply.

"So stubborn. Nothing ever changes." He kissed me, and I felt myself sinking. Then it was Oliver sinking—to his knees in front of me. Pushing up my dress. Pulling down my underwear.

I think I whimpered. I dropped my phone.

He laughed as he tossed one of my legs over his shoulder, and I felt his breath on me. "Don't worry. I promise I'm going to be very, very gentle."

And he *was* gentle—soft kisses up my inner thighs; sweet, lingering strokes with his tongue up my center; slow, dizzying spirals over my clit.

I flattened my palms against the door and struggled not to make the kind of embarrassing noises you heard through hotel room walls.

Then he *wasn't* gentle—flicking the tip of his tongue over my clit in a quick, fluttering motion that made my lower body hum; sucking it into his mouth and moaning with delight; clutching my thigh with one hand as he fucked me with two fingers on the other.

I clapped a palm over my mouth. I banged on the door. I felt my legs begin to shudder and go numb with pleasure, the one I stood on about to buckle.

"Oliver," I panted. "I can't stand up. I can't stand up."

He laughed, but he didn't let up, and within ten seconds, my entire body was convulsing, wave after wave of pure pleasure rippling out from his tongue to the tips of my toes and the ends of my hair and my tingling breasts that ached to be touched. It was the most intense, most otherworldly, most powerful orgasm I'd ever experienced, and it made me want *more*.

I wanted Oliver to fuck me. I *craved* it. And he had to be hard, right? He had to want it just as badly as I did.

Suddenly I heard a beeping noise, like a phone alarm going off.

"Yes!" Oliver fist-pumped and picked up my cell from the floor. "Under five minutes. I win."

I pulled my leg off his shoulder, the sultry haze around me evaporating. "Huh?"

He looked up at me triumphantly. "I made you come in under five minutes."

My mouth fell open. There were so many things wrong with what he'd said, I could hardly think. "Wait a minute. Wait a minute." I put out a hand. "You set a timer?"

He shrugged. "Yeah."

"On *my* phone?"

"Yeah."

I shook my head. "How did you even—"

"Your passcode is your birthday." He gave me an admonishing look. "You should really be more careful."

"But … I didn't even notice you playing with it."

"I know. I'm good, right?"

I brought my legs together. Tight. "You are vile and loathsome. And I never took any bet."

He burst out laughing. "Doesn't matter. It was more of a challenge I set for myself. Under five minutes." He wiped his mouth and sat back. "Damn, I'm good."

I wanted to punch him. *For giving me an orgasm.* What the fuck was going on?

"This whole thing was a ruse, wasn't it?" I demanded. "You were never worried you didn't know what you were doing with women. Or that they were faking it."

"Fuck no," he scoffed. "I didn't go to Harvard, but I know my stuff."

I shook my head. "You were just mad you hadn't made me come."

"Yeah, pretty much."

"I cannot believe I actually had warm, fuzzy feelings toward you tonight."

"Aww." He put a hand on his heart. "That's cute."

"Fuck you."

He put his hands on the button of his shorts. "I mean … we *can*. *I'm* certainly willing and able."

"Fuck. You." I yanked the door open, grabbed my phone from the floor, and took off down the hall, without shoes, without underwear, without dignity.

And I swore—I *swore*—to myself that I would never let Oliver Ford Pemberton get near me again.

It was a promise I couldn't keep.

What was *wrong* with me?

Twelve

Oliver

NOW

I RELAXED. THAT COULD NOT HAVE GONE BETTER.

Beside me, Chloe was talking a mile a minute about the marketing possibilities of our heritage whiskey—what we might call it, the potential for ad campaigns, the label on the bottle, the price point—and I could hear in her voice how thrilled she was with the idea.

"And you're positive the farmers are going to sell to you?" she asked, her brows knit together.

"Well, at this point, there are only two full-time commercial farmers left on the island," I told her. "A father and son by the name of Jergen and Josef Feldmann—Jacob and Rebecca's grandson and great-grandson. Both widowed, still living in the original house. They grow *some* Feldmann rye right now, but not a ton of it."

"Incredible," she marveled. "And you've spoken to them?"

"Several times. They're willing to increase production right away and devote several hundred acres exclusively to Feldmann rye. They'll plant it this fall."

"Really? They agreed to it just like that?"

"Uh, not exactly." I readjusted my cap on my head. "See, they're looking to get out of the farming business in the next few years. Jergen's getting older, and Josef has a bad leg. They had a buyer all ready to give them top dollar for their land, too. Some automotive tycoon who wants to build a vacation house."

Chloe recoiled. "Fuck that. He can't have our land."

I laughed. "That's the thing. It's not ours. Not *yet*, anyway."

"What do you mean?"

"I mean, in order to secure the land for our purposes, I had to offer to purchase it outright."

Her jaw dropped. "You mean, not just buy the rye from the Feldmanns but the farm itself? Won't that be expensive?"

"Uh, yeah. I had to promise to come close to what the tycoon was offering, which was almost a million."

Her jaw fell open. "Sheesh." Then she grinned and thumped the tops of my legs. "But that's like a drop in the bucket for you, right? And what better investment for your inheritance than land? It's not like it will lose its value, right?"

I cleared my throat. "I hope not."

"So did you agree on a price?"

"I think we're close."

"And you need me to seal the deal, eh?" She elbowed me in the ribs. "Not to worry, I can charm anyone into anything. My dad always says I could sell sand to the beach."

"Good. Because I'll definitely need your help. Not only do we need them to agree to our price, but we need them to stay on for at least the first few seasons. I'm no farmer."

"Can we find a tenant farmer?"

"You want to trust our precious Russian rye to a tenant farmer who doesn't know the land?" I asked her.

"I see your point." She was quiet a minute. "I'm sure for the right amount of money, they can be persuaded to stay. We'll just have to make sure it's worth their while. Good thing you have deep pockets."

I coughed. "Right."

"We're almost there, look!"

Up ahead, the island's tree-lined, rocky shore grew nearer. Chloe continue to bubble with excitement as we docked, lifting her heavy pack and slipping it onto her back as though it weighed nothing at all. I was surprised she didn't start skipping down the gangplank. Once we arrived on the island, I completed our camper registration and showed a ranger the permit I'd purchased at the Fishtown dock.

I was feeling a little guilty about how happy and hopeful Chloe was about this trip and the farm—after all, I hadn't exactly told her the *entire* truth. But I'd thought about it a lot beforehand, and I'd come to the conclusion that it would be better to sort of let the truth trickle out in small increments rather than lay it on her all at once. If I'd done that, she'd have only focused on the downsides and completely ignored all the opportunity. This way, I gave her a chance to grow attached to the idea of the distillery and our heritage rye … so attached I was hoping she'd do anything to have it.

"So what should we do first?" I asked her. "It's three-thirty. Our meeting with the Feldmanns is at seven. I set it up for later because I wasn't sure which ferry we'd be able to catch."

Chloe nodded. "So should we hike first? Check out the lighthouse? Maybe take a swim?"

"Sure. Actually, that's perfect because the farm is on the north side of the island, which isn't far from our campsite. We can end up there."

She beamed. "Let's do it."

Chloe remained in high spirits on the half-mile hike along the boardwalk to the lighthouse, on the 117-step spiral climb to the top, and as we stood on the top of the observation deck taking in the incredible view.

"God, it's so beautiful," she said, the wind whipping at her hair, her voice full of awe. "I can see why the tycoon wants a vacation house here."

I thought of the price the tycoon was willing to pay—the price that I was going to have to match—and nearly made a joke about jumping. But I didn't want her to get suspicious that I didn't have the money. "It is beautiful."

She sighed. "I don't think I could ever live anywhere too far from the water."

"Me either."

"But sometimes I miss the hustle of the city, you know? I did like Chicago. That had water and hustle."

"Chicago is awesome," I agreed.

"But my roots are up here," she said firmly. "And I like working for my family."

"You're lucky your passion matched up with your family business," I said. "I've got no interest whatsoever in soap, toothpaste, and laundry detergent."

"Do your parents still pressure you to work for the company?" she asked.

"Not really. They have Hughie, after all, the golden

child. What do they need with me?"

"Oh, come on." She elbowed me. "Your parents adore you. *My* parents adore you. You've always been the one with all the charm. Nothing against Hughie, of course, but he's about as charming as a bar of soap."

I laughed. "True. And as squeaky clean. He never did anything wrong. Never got in any trouble."

"That's because he was boring and unimaginative. Give me trouble any day."

I looked over at her. "Still?"

She shrugged and laughed a little. "Old habits are hard to break. I've learned to deal more … productively with some of my impulses, but I still crave chaos. I don't like to sit still, don't like taking no for an answer, I'll argue about anything, and I often act without thinking things through. Although my therapist is trying to help me with that."

"You have a therapist?" I was surprised she'd shared that kind of personal detail. Chloe seemed so determined to put up a front where I was concerned—the admission allowed a little vulnerability to seep through. Her honesty made me feel worse.

"Yeah. His name is Ken." She grinned ruefully. "I started seeing him a few years ago after another relationship ended badly, to try to sort out some things in my head, maybe discover why I'm always attracted to dickheads."

"Did you figure it out?"

She shrugged. "Ken thinks I go for guys I know will disappoint me. I set myself up for failure so I don't really have to put myself out there. *I* think I just have shitty taste in men." Then she laughed. "But it doesn't really matter anyway, because I'm so busy at Cloverleigh now, especially with my father on the verge of retiring. I don't really have time to date. Should we head down?"

Without waiting for me to answer, she turned and started the descent down the spiral staircase.

When we reached the bottom, we decided to take a trail leading west toward the shipwreck of the Morazan, visible in the water from the south shore of the island, and the Valley of the Giants, a grove of massive, old-growth cedar trees.

"So your dad is retiring, huh?" I asked, walking next to her on the sandy dirt path. "Will he promote you as his replacement? He sort of gave me that impression when we spoke last month."

"I don't know for sure," she said, staring at her feet. "I hope so. My dad's been so reluctant to retire we haven't talked much about it in any detail. But it would make sense, since April has no interest in anything beyond weddings, and we're the only two siblings who work there anymore."

"What would be the reason if he didn't promote you?"

She sighed. "Who knows? I think I've proven myself where work is concerned, but sometimes I feel like he looks at me and still sees the smart-mouthed teenager who ignored curfew, bent rules, and didn't give a shit what people said. Maybe he's worried I'll make too many changes and not respect tradition."

"I don't know about that," I said, reaching ahead of her to move a branch in our way. "I get the feeling he trusts your instincts and appreciates your work ethic. I've seen the increased sales and visibility of Cloverleigh wines over the past several years. I think you've proven yourself."

"Thanks." She gave me a smile. "I was thinking the other day that if I do get promoted, I'd probably move back to Cloverleigh, maybe into Frannie's old apartment over the garage, now that she's moved into Mack's house."

I whistled. "Move back home? You're brave."

"Well, I'd like to be on site more, and I think my parents are planning to travel a lot, so they won't be breathing down my neck all the time. That's my hope, anyway."

We walked a little further in silence, slapping at the occasional mosquito, pulling out water bottles for the occasional sip.

"Tell me about Frannie and Mack. He's the CFO, right?" I asked.

"Right. They started dating over the winter and just got engaged a couple weeks ago. He's a single dad of three girls that Frannie absolutely adores. They're perfect for each other and totally in love. I think she wants to get married this fall."

"Wow. That's fast."

She looked over at me with mischief in her grin. "That's kind of the way it's supposed to be, Oliver. You get engaged so you can get married."

Somehow I had veered into dangerous territory, and I tried to back out of it. "Can I borrow your sunscreen? I think the back of my neck is getting burned."

"Sure." She grabbed a can of SPF 30 from a side pocket of her pack. "Want me to do it?"

"Okay." I turned around and let her spray me, hoping she'd forget about the topic of engagement.

Nope.

"So whatever happened to *your* fiancée?" she asked as we started moving again. "What was her name? Alice? Ellen?"

"Alison."

"Alison. Right." When I didn't say more, she poked again. "So where's Alison now?"

"In Chicago, I assume. With her new husband."

Chloe stopped walking. "She left you for someone else?"

"No. I broke it off."

"Why?"

"Because it was never going to work. I wasn't who she thought I was," I said, continuing to move along the path.

Chloe hurried to catch up. "Who did she think you were?"

I wasn't sure how to answer that without giving everything away. "Probably my brother Hughie."

She snorted. "So she wanted someone stuffy and predictable?"

"She wanted a certain kind of life. She wanted to get married, quit her job, and move into a house like Hughie and Lisa's, where she'd have a housekeeper, chef, and personal trainer at her fingertips." I stared at the ground as we walked for a moment. "When we first started dating, I think she hoped I'd play around with the distillery for a while and then get serious and go to work for Pemberton. Join the country club. Buy a yacht. I could tell she felt let down when that didn't happen. Also, she told me so constantly."

"She sounds really fucking terrible, Oliver. You should be glad you're not married to her."

"Believe me, I am."

"Why'd you propose to her in the first place?"

I kicked a rock on the path. "She said it was time. My parents said it was time. My grandmother said she wasn't getting any younger. And my brother made me feel like I was a fuckup. I guess I was trying to show them I wasn't." I was silent for a moment. "But as it turns out, I was."

She elbowed me. "Stop. You're not a fuckup."

"No?"

"No," she scoffed. "You've got everything, Oliver. A successful business, a great family, probably a cool apartment and a million friends. You made the right decision by not marrying the wrong person, you give back by teaching sailing to underprivileged kids, and you're even marginally attractive. What about that says fuckup?"

I laughed, giving her the side eye. "Marginally attractive, huh?"

"Sure. I mean, you could use a haircut, and your gut could be all soft and flabby for all I know, but objectively speaking, I'd say you're okay."

"Gee, thanks. But I assure you …" I cut her off and stood directly in front of her so she walked right into my chest. I had to grab her arms to keep her from falling backward. "There's nothing soft and flabby about me. Feel free to check."

She glanced down at the space between our bodies and then met my eyes again. Her cheeks colored slightly. "I'll take your word for it. Let's keep going."

Thirteen

Chloe

NOW

AFTER SEEING THE PARTIALLY SUBMERGED WRECK OF THE Morazan, we hiked through a grove of giant cedars and continued along the trail that led up onto the bluffs along the western shore of the island. The wind was strong but the sun was blistering hot, and the blue water of Lake Michigan glittered beckoningly. I was sweltering—and every time I thought about slamming into Oliver's broad chest, I felt hotter.

I needed to cool off.

"What do you think?" I asked Oliver. "Do we have time to go down and swim before we head over to the farm?"

He checked his wristwatch. "Yeah. We're good."

Carefully, we made our way down to the water, and ditched our packs, boots, hats, sunglasses, and clothing on the sand. I pulled out my tube of facial sunscreen again, reapplied to my face, then took out the can. "Hey, can you spray my back?" I asked him.

"Sure." He took the can and did as I asked, and I

wondered if he was looking at my butt or keeping his eyes where they belonged.

"Thanks," I said when he was done. "Now let me spray you or you're going to be in pain all night long and you'll keep me up with your complaining."

He rolled his eyes but allowed me to spray his back and shoulders before he took the can again and sprayed his chest and face.

"Oliver! You're not supposed to spray that on your face, I have a better one for that," I scolded.

"What's the difference?" He tossed the can onto the sand, then took off running toward the water. "Race you! Last one in's a rotten egg!"

"No fair, you had a head start!" I yelled as I followed close behind. The water was freezing, and I squealed as I rushed in waist-deep.

Oliver dove under first, and before he came up, I took a second to make sure my bikini top was properly in place before dunking myself. When I popped up, he was right there grinning at me, his hair sticking out in all directions.

"I win," he announced.

I splashed him. "Not everything has to be a competition. If we're going to be partners, we need to work better together."

"You're right," he said, surprising me.

I squinted at him. "Did the cold water freeze your brain or something?"

"Not at all." He stood up, the water hitting him at the top of his shorts, which hung a little lower than they had before. "I just agree with you that we need to put our usual differences and competitive streaks aside. We're a team now."

I tilted my head. "I guess we are."

"Does that mean your answer is yes? You *will* go into business with me?"

I was tempted to say yes right then and there. Oliver *had* something with this whole Russian rye angle, and I was eager to jump on board. But I'd eagerly jumped on Oliver's board without thinking before, and it had not ended well for me. Although truth be told, he looked so good standing there, the sun glinting off his wet skin, his blue eyes bright, water droplets running down his washboard abs to the top of his V lines … for a moment, I'd have jumped aboard anything he wanted me too.

But I caught myself. I wasn't that girl anymore. "I'm still thinking."

"What are you thinking about?"

I realized I was still staring at his abdomen and lifted my eyes to his. He was grinning. He'd *so* caught me staring at his nether regions.

"Nothing," I said quickly, ducking under the water up to my neck. My nipples were hard.

"I don't believe you." He moved a little closer. "If we're going to be partners and all, we should be truthful with each other, right?"

"Ha! I'm not the one with a history of obscuring the truth. And anyway, being truthful doesn't mean we have to tell each other everything." I swam backward as he approached. "It just means we don't *lie* to each other."

"I was only asking a question, Chloe. What are you getting so defensive about?"

I forced myself to stop retreating. If this thing with us was going to work, I could not let him push me around. "Frankly, I was thinking about all the bad decisions I've made in your company."

Oliver tossed his head back and laughed. "Some of those decisions were *totally* yours, I'd like to remind you. I'm thinking about one in particular, a certain night in my college dorm."

"I'm not blaming you entirely, I'm only saying that I have a history of questionable judgment where you're concerned," I said.

"You liked the games just as much as I did. Admit it."

"Maybe I did." I focused on my hand fanning through the water. "I like to think that I'm smarter now. More mature."

"I don't know, you seemed pretty mature that night." He fell onto his back, floating on the surface. "You knew what you'd come for, and you got it."

"Um, as we have established, *you* were the only one to come that night."

He stood up. "Oh, that is cold. There I was, doing *you* a favor—"

"Ha!" I shrieked, splashing him. "As if it was such a hardship for you!"

"That was a lot of pressure, being your first," he argued. "I don't think you've ever appreciated that. If I didn't give you a good experience, you might have been scarred for life."

"Well, don't worry. The experience was fine. I hardly felt a thing, and it was over before I knew it."

"That's it." Oliver lunged for me, trying to dunk me beneath the surface. "When are you going to stop teasing me about that?"

"When it stops being funny, so never!"

He finally succeeded in shoving me under, but I clung to his neck so hard we both ended up fully submerged.

Underwater, we each struggled to hold the other one down, just like we had a hundred times before as kids. Eventually, we burst above the surface again, laughing and gasping for air, my arms still looped around his neck.

I let go of him immediately and backed up as I caught my breath. "No fair," I panted. "You're a lot bigger than me."

"And you have nails," he said, checking out the red marks I'd left on his arm. "I forgot how you used to scratch me."

"Let's call it even." I ducked under once more so I could get my hair off my face. When I opened my eyes again, he was staring at me.

"What?" I asked.

"We go back a long way, don't we?"

I shrugged. "Since we were born. I'd say that's a pretty long way."

"And even though we've had our differences, if there was something one of us needed, like *really* needed, we'd help each other out, right?"

"Right." I paused. "What's this about? Do you need a kidney or something?"

He smiled. "No. I was just thinking that I'm really lucky to have you in my life. No matter what happens with the business, I hope you know you can always come to me if you need something. I'll always be there for you."

A little shiver moved up my spine. "Thanks. That might be the nicest thing you've ever said to me."

"I mean it. I know our friendship hasn't exactly been conventional, or even consistent, but I care about you, Chloe."

"You do?" Who the hell was this guy? He didn't sound at all like the Oliver I knew. It was disorienting and highly suspicious—but … it was nice too.

"Yeah. You cross my mind all the time."

"Well, thanks. I care about you too." I hesitated before going on. "I've spent years being angry with you, and it feels nice to let that go."

The smile he gave me was sweet and boyish. It made my stomach do quick, fluttery things, and I had to look away.

"So what do you say we continue on?" he suggested. "Maybe sit on the beach a little to dry off, eat something, and then head inland?"

"Sounds good."

We made our way back to the sand and sat down to let the sun and warm breeze dry us off. We ate our sandwiches and chatted a little more about the rye, about what buildings we'd need at Cloverleigh and where they might go, how many people we might have to hire, when all of this might happen, how expensive it would be.

"I'm sorry I don't have money to invest," I said, pulling my hair into a ponytail. "But I could look into getting a loan if that would help us."

"Leave the money to me," he said confidently. "We won't have to deal with loans or banks."

After getting dressed and applying another layer of bug spray and sunscreen—I would be glad when I finally got a real shower—we slipped our packs on our backs again. Retracing our steps back along the trail the way we'd come, we took a left after passing the shipwreck. The trail leading inland cut across the island's center and took us past Florence Lake, the ruins of an old cabin, and the one-room schoolhouse where Rebecca Hofstadt Feldmann had taught, complete with a bell on top. We left the trail to peek in the windows, but they were boarded up.

"What do you think of naming the whiskey after her?" I suggested as we continued on. "Rebecca's Rye."

"Rebecca's Rye." Oliver thought for a moment. "I like it. It has a nice, alliterative ring to it. I wonder if she had brown eyes."

"I bet we can find out. Maybe the Feldmanns will even have a photograph of her," I said excitedly. "Although it would for sure be in black and white. But if it's good, maybe we could even use it on the label. With the family's permission, of course."

"We can ask. I like the idea." He elbowed me playfully. "Are we partners yet?"

I sighed. "I suppose we are."

"Finally! I was starting to get worried."

"Really?"

"Truth? Nah. I knew you'd come around."

I elbowed him back. "When we get back home, Oliver, we need a contract laying out exactly how this partnership is going to work. I don't want to work *for* you, I want to work *with* you. We're equals in this, and we both bring value to the table."

"Absolutely," he said. "We'll work it out. Do you want to become a partner in Brown Eyed Girl Spirits? Or would you prefer to form a new LLC for anything produced at Cloverleigh?"

I stopped walking and grabbed his arm, making him face me. "You'd bring me on as a partner in Brown Eyed Girl?"

"Sure. If that's what you want." He hesitated. "That's what *I* want."

"It is?"

"Of course. I shouldn't have done it without you in the first place. And I'm sorry. I'll always be sorry for that. Brown Eyed Girl was always supposed to be *our* thing. I was wrong to do it alone." He put his hands on my shoulders. "It's named for you. You should be part of it."

Meeting his eyes, I wondered if he, like me, was thinking of the night he came up with the name. My pulse started to race.

"Say yes, Chloe," he urged. "Let's do everything together."

But I couldn't say anything at that moment. All I could do was stare at Oliver's mouth and think about what a good kisser he was. I felt hot and dizzy, assaulted by memories of being skin to skin with him, his body moving over mine. My vision started to cloud as his words circled through my head.

Let's do everything together.

I took a step back. I'd been at this crossroads before and made the wrong choice. I couldn't get swept away again. "Okay, that sounds good."

"Great. When we get to Detroit, I'll set up a meeting with my financial advisor, and we'll make it official on paper." He offered a hand. "Partners in everything?"

I put my hand in his and shook it, wishing I could blame the heat for the erratic way my heart was beating. "Partners in everything."

We made it to the Feldmann farm by about six-thirty and knocked on the front door of the house—an old, weather-beaten, two-story structure with flaking white paint, a sagging front porch, and a black-shingled roof. Our knock was answered by a stout, pot-bellied guy whose bushy beard was about half gray. He wore a yellow T-shirt advertising a charter fishing business in Wisconsin, and his skin was ruddy from years in the sun.

"You the guy from Detroit?" he asked Oliver.

"I am." Oliver held out his hand. "I'm Oliver Pemberton, and this is my business partner, Chloe Sawyer."

"Nice to meet you. Josef Feldmann." He shook hands with both of us. "Come on in. Dad's in the back."

We followed him into the house, which was cluttered but clean. I noticed Josef walked with a limp.

"Dad's a little hard of hearing, so you'll have to speak a bit louder if you want him to hear you." Josef shook his head as he led us through a small, dated kitchen—the latest upgrade appeared to be a Formica countertop—adding, "He refuses to wear his hearing aids, the damn fool."

"No problem," Oliver said.

"The back" turned out to be a small den, which had been added onto the house sometime after it was built. Jergen Feldmann was sitting on a beat-up recliner watching Jeopardy on television at an absurdly high volume.

"Dad?" said Josef loudly. "They're here."

"What?" The old guy blinked at us through thick-lensed glasses.

Josef muted the television. "The people who want to make an offer on the farm are here," he shouted.

"Oh." Jergen struggled to get out of his chair.

"Don't get up," I said clearly, moving into the room and offering him my hand. "Hello. I'm Chloe Sawyer."

He shook it. "Jergen Feldmann."

Oliver introduced himself as well, and Josef gestured to the sofa. "Please sit down. Can I offer you something to drink?"

"No, thank you," I said.

He smiled. "Not even a little taste of whiskey made from our rye?"

My eyes widened. "You have some?"

"Sure, we do. We've been making our own moonshine here for generations."

Oliver and I exchanged a glance. "Why not?" I returned Josef's smile. "We'll try it."

The whiskey was rough, but it had a distinctive, unique flavor that both Oliver and I loved. I knew with the right equipment and process, we had the potential to create something that would taste extraordinary. After chatting (loudly) with the Feldmanns about their farm and family history, Josef asked us if we'd like to take a walk around the farm.

We took him up on his offer, and if I hadn't been sold on the idea of buying this land before tasting the whiskey made from the rye that grew there, I was now. Maybe it was the slight buzz I had, maybe it was the beauty of the fields in the early evening light, maybe it was the growing excitement I felt about being a part of this story, but I *knew* we had to have that land.

"Have you given any thought to my offer?" Oliver asked Josef as we circled back toward the house. It felt glorious to walk without the weight of the pack on my back.

"Yeah. Yeah, we've discussed it." Josef scratched the back of his neck. "The other offer is higher, you know, but Dad likes yours better."

"It's cash up front," Oliver explained to me. "They can stay in the house as long as they want."

"And he doesn't much like the idea of someone tearing down the house and carving up the farm," Josef said. "My great-great grandfather built this house and raised that barn. My great-grandmother taught school at that schoolhouse up the road. Their bones are buried right over there in the cemetery. We don't want all that erased." He sighed. "But it's hard to say no to more money."

"It is," I agreed, turning on the charm. "But there are some things money can't buy, and a legacy is one of them. In fact, your family's history is a huge part of what we want to do here. We plan to not only keep it alive, but celebrate it. We were even thinking of naming the whiskey we make after your great-great grandmother—Rebecca's Rye. If it's okay with you and your dad, of course. We wondered if we could see a picture of her?"

Within an hour, Josef was shaking our hands, telling us we had a deal. We celebrated with a little more moonshine, promised to get in touch next week, and left with the Feldmanns' assurance that the land would be ours as soon as we wanted it and they'd stay on long enough to get the rye planted in the fall.

Oliver and I walked away from the house, barely able to contain our excitement. "Oh my God," I whispered as we moved quickly down the long dirt driveway. "It's really happening!"

"Fuck yes, it is." Oliver poked my shoulder playfully. "You totally made that happen."

"Me! No, I didn't—your offer is what made that happen."

"But you saw how he was hesitating because the other guy's offer was higher, and you swooped in there with all that talk about carrying on his family's legacy and naming the rye after Rebecca and asking to see her picture. Your timing was perfect."

I laughed. "It was a team effort—our first one!"

"And I'd say it was an unqualified success." He grabbed my hand and squeezed it. "We make a good team."

My heart raced ahead of my breath for a moment, and heat blossomed in my cheeks. "Should we head to the campsite?"

"Yes. It's getting dark and the bugs will be even worse pretty soon. I want to get our tent set up."

The tent. That's right.

I had to share a tent with Oliver tonight. Sleep next to him. Hear him breathing. Talk to him quietly in the dark.

Earlier today I'd been worried about him keeping to his side of the tent, but now I found myself wondering how I'd react if he didn't.

We walked the mile to the campground in no particular hurry, holding hands the whole way.

Fourteen

Oliver

NOW

The Popple campground was the farthest site from the docks, therefore the least crowded. In my opinion, it was also the most beautiful. Located on a sandy bluff, it had the benefit of the lake breeze to keep the mosquitoes at bay, and the beach at the bottom of the dune was sandy and secluded. I'd camped here a couple times last summer when I was scouting the farms, and it was by far my favorite.

"What do you think?" I asked Chloe when it was clear we'd have our pick of the seven possible sites. There was no one else around. "Base of the dune or up here?"

Chloe slapped at a bug on her arm. "Which will have less mosquitoes?"

I laughed. "Those are everywhere, but these two sites are higher on the bluff, and maybe the elevation will give us a stronger wind."

"Then let's stay up here."

I dropped the pack from my back and attached our

permit to the post at site number 7. "Here it is. I'll get started on the tent."

She grimaced as she glanced at the outhouse. "I should have used the bathroom at the Feldmann's. Or not drunk whiskey."

I grinned as I unzipped my pack. "You're a tough cookie. You'll survive."

As I set up the tent, I thought about the day so far. Everything had gone perfectly—the Feldmanns had given their word they'd accept our offer, Chloe was on board with everything, and the two of us were getting along even better than I'd expected. In fact, I was having a hell of a lot of fun with her.

That hadn't been part of the plan.

But it hadn't been bullshit, what I'd said to her about us. I did think of her as someone who'd always be there for me, and I'd always be there for her. We ran hot and cold, but we had history. We'd shared some unforgettable experiences, both painful and pleasurable. But beneath all the surface-level ups and downs was a bond that couldn't be broken. I felt it in my gut, and I had to believe Chloe did too. Otherwise, after everything that had gone down between us, why would she be here with me?

We made the perfect team. We'd challenge each other to be better, smarter, more creative. We wouldn't pull punches or cut corners. We each brought unique knowledge and experience to the venture, and we'd known each other so long, we communicated almost in shorthand.

The problem was our physical chemistry.

No matter how much we fought it, it was always there, simmering just below the surface of everything we said, threatening to erupt at any moment. I wasn't sure I could stop it, even if I wanted to. Even if I knew it would only make things more complicated.

Because it would.

"Want help?" she asked when she got back. How she managed to look so beautiful after a day of hiking in this hot, humid weather was beyond me.

"Sure."

Together we set up camp, had a snack, and tied the remains of our food up out of reach of the chipmunks. "We need more water," she said, wiping her forehead. "And I could use a swim. Want to go down to the beach? We can bring some water back for purifying."

"Good idea," I said. "And I've got a little something besides water in the meantime." From my pack, I pulled out a flask I'd filled with my favorite bourbon.

She laughed. "Of course you do."

I offered her the first sip, then I took two before sticking it back into my pack.

"Come on," she said. "I'll race you."

Since we still had our suits on, we took off running for the beach and didn't stop until we hit the sand, where we tore off clothing and dashed into the cool, clear water. I beat her by a full five seconds because one of her bootlaces was tied in a knot.

"I don't know why you even challenge me," I teased her. "You've never once beaten me."

"I totally could have won that time," she insisted. "I had a wardrobe malfunction. I made it down to the beach just as fast as you did."

"*Maybe,*" I allowed. "I guess I could call the race to the beach a tie. I'm feeling generous."

"Well, thank you very much." She stuck her tongue

out at me before ducking beneath the water again. "God, this feels good," she said when she surfaced. "It was so hot today."

"It was." I tried to keep my eyes off her breasts. "But it will cool off soon. The sun is going down fast. Clouds are rolling in."

We stayed in the water and watched it happen, the sky turning orange and then pink as the sun slid lower on the horizon and disappeared into the lake. Afterward, it was immediately cooler.

Chloe looked up and down the beach. "Guess we have the place to ourselves, huh?"

"We do. So feel free to skinny dip if you'd like."

"Ha. You wish." She backstroked by me with perfect form.

"Show-off. You still swim a lot?"

"I belong to a gym. Sometimes I swim before work. It's good exercise."

"You look good doing it."

"Thanks." She turned around and stroked back toward me. When she got close, she ducked under and then stood up, tilting her head back to get her hair off her face, water streaming down her body.

"You look good, period," I told her, unable to stop staring at her curves, her skin, her taut little nipples poking through the fabric of her bikini top. My dick started to get hard.

She didn't say anything for a moment. "Oliver, what did you mean earlier, when you said I cross your mind?"

"I meant that I've thought about you." I moved closer to her, drawn by some invisible force. "I still think about you."

She backed up. "Did you think about me when you left

for Europe without even saying goodbye? When you ignored my texts and phone calls? When you came home and started a distillery without me?"

"Yes. I know you don't believe me, but I did."

"All you had to do was text me back. *'Decided to move to Europe and party for two years instead of go into business with you. Peace out.'*"

"I'm sorry. I should have."

"I still don't understand why you didn't."

"I was young and stupid, Chloe. I wasn't ready to handle what I felt for you after that weekend. I panicked."

"You said things. I thought you meant them."

"I did. I just …" Seeing how hurt she was even after all this time cinched my heart. "Freaked out. I'm sorry." I got close enough to her to take her by the shoulders. "I meant every word I said that weekend. And I mean what I'm saying to you now—you're special to me."

She looked away from me, toward the horizon. "We can't keep doing this every time we see each other. It … messes with me. Every time I think I know what we are, what this is, how we feel, it blows up in my face."

"It messes with me too. I left Chicago—fuck, I left the *country*, so I could try to forget you." I squeezed her arms. "But I never did."

"We're going into business together, Oliver. We can't be more than friends."

I took her chin in my hand, forcing her to look at me. "We've always been more than friends."

She didn't argue.

Unable to resist, I pressed my lips to her forehead, her cheek, her jaw.

"This is a terrible, terrible idea," she said weakly.

"I know." I moved my mouth down her throat.

"One of us needs to be rational and stop this before it starts."

"Definitely." I pulled her body tighter against mine, and she shivered. "Are you cold?"

"No. I just … *felt you*, and I got excited." Then she pushed me back. "But that's enough."

Inwardly groaning, I held up my hands and backed up. "Sorry."

We looked at each other under the darkening sky, our skin blanketed with goosebumps. "We're not kids anymore," she said softly. "We have to be mature and think about the bigger picture. The long-term success of Brown Eyed Girl is more important than short-term gratification, right?"

"Right," I said. "But in the future, we should definitely not hold business meetings in our bathing suits. Your body is killing me."

She folded her arms over her chest and gave me a sly grin, her eyes half-shut. "Good."

We each collected some water, purified it, and cleaned up. I gave Chloe the privacy of the tent while I took advantage of the empty woods to strip naked and give myself a quick, frigid bath. I dressed in shorts and a clean T-shirt as fast as I could, trying not to become a mosquito feast, and used a little more clean water to brush my teeth. From the west, I heard the distant roll of thunder, which surprised me. I hadn't seen any storms on the radar.

I called out to Chloe. "Can I come in?"

"Yes." She unzipped the tent. "I just want to brush my teeth, but I'll do it out there. Was that thunder?"

"Yeah. A summer storm must have popped up." I saw the worried look on her face. "But probably just a small one."

We switched places, and she was gone for only a minute or two before hustling back inside. "I saw some lightning. You're sure we'll be okay in here if it storms?"

"Positive," I told her, trying not to dwell on the fact that she didn't appear to be wearing shorts beneath her large T-shirt. "But let's move all our stuff inside. We'll have a little less room for sleeping, but we don't want wet gear." We gathered everything up and got it inside the tent just as the first fat raindrops began to fall. The thunder grew louder.

"It's so dark all of a sudden," she said nervously. "Did you pack a light?"

I pulled a small LED lantern from my pack and switched it on, setting it in one corner of the tent. "There. Better?"

"Yes."

"I'd forgotten you were afraid of the dark," I teased, tossing my flip-flops aside.

"I'm not afraid," she said, tucking hers behind her pack. "I just don't like it. Same way you don't like ketchup."

"Ketchup is disgusting. The dark is fun."

"I just like knowing there's light if I need it. Especially out here in the middle of the woods. And with a storm coming."

"Don't worry, Dimples. I'll protect you from anything threatening." I dug out my flask from my bag and handed it to her.

"And who's going to protect me from you?" she asked, raising her eyebrows as she uncapped the flask and lifted it to her lips.

"Does that mean you didn't pack the frying pan?"

"I must have forgotten." She narrowed her eyes and handed the flask back to me. "But don't think that means you can mess with me tonight. You promised."

"That's true. I did."

"And you said I could trust you."

"You can." After another sip, I gave the bourbon back to her. "So tell me all your secrets."

She giggled and took another sip. "No way. You forget, I know you."

"Then let's play a game. Truth or dare."

Pausing with the flask halfway to her lips, she gave me a disapproving look. "Not doing that either. You'll dare me to take off my clothes or something."

"I swear to God, I will be a perfect gentleman." As rain began to pelt the outside of the tent, I lay down on my side atop my sleeping bag, propped on one elbow. "But we can take out the dare part of it, and just ask each other questions. You can start."

She took another sip of bourbon. "Shouldn't we talk about business?"

"I'm giving us the night off." Outside, the thunder rumbled loudly. "Go ahead."

"Hmm." She stared at the flask and swirled it around. "If you could change something about yourself, what would it be?"

I thought for a moment. "I wish I could see the future."

She gave me an exasperated look. "Oliver. That's not how you're supposed to answer that question."

"Okay, fine." I exhaled and gave it ten more seconds. "I'm working on being more responsible. More mature."

"Oh yeah?"

"Yeah. I think a lot of the mistakes I've made in my life are because I've never really thought long-term about anything. I made every decision based on how I felt in the moment." I frowned. "Unlike Hughie, who did everything right from the start."

She handed the flask back to me. "I get that. I used to feel that way about my older sisters. Like the three of them had all been these perfect angels, and I was born with horns on my head. My parents never knew what to make of me." She gathered her damp hair over one shoulder. "After a while, I think I just acted out because it was expected of me. It was what set me apart."

I nodded. "Okay, my turn. Let me think. What do you want most in life?"

"What do I want most? Hmm." She played with the frayed hem of her T-shirt. "I want to prove myself. I don't just want to take over the family business and run it like he would. I want to make my own mark. Like with our distillery."

I loved that she called it *our* distillery. "I have no doubt you can do all those things. Do you doubt yourself?"

"Sometimes," she admitted.

"Well, it never shows."

Her cheeks grew a little pink in the soft light. "Thanks."

"So those are your professional goals. What about personal goals? Do you want a family?"

She inhaled and exhaled. "I don't know. I've thought about it. I guess I've just never come to any conclusions, and I've never met anyone I was dying to have kids with, so …" She shrugged. "It's never really been at the top of my list. What about you?"

We traded the flask again. "I've always assumed I would

get married and have kids. In my family, it's just what you do when you get to be a certain age. It's tradition."

She nodded. "Tradition seems really important in your family."

"It is. Especially to my grandmother, and she's got a lot of influence."

"Why is that?"

"Because she still controls the money."

"Really? I thought you inherited your money when you turned twenty-five. I saw you in Chicago right after that, and I remember you saying you'd just gotten access to it."

I tipped back some bourbon. "I did inherit a portion of my trust after grad school, but the Pemberton family fortune is still controlled by Gran. And our trusts were set up in a way that they sort of trickle into our names as we get older and hit certain milestones."

"So what are the milestones?"

"Turning twenty-five. Getting married. Buying a home. Having kids. She wants to see that we're settled before we inherit. I mean, she's ninety. She has pretty traditional, old-fashioned values." Fuck—I hadn't meant to get into this with Chloe yet. The bourbon was loosening my tongue. "Whose turn is it?"

"Mine, I think." She took the flask from me and tipped it up. "God, this is good. I better stop drinking it though. I really don't want to visit that outhouse again tonight, especially in the rain. Here, take it. I'm done."

I took one last drink from it and screwed the top back on before setting it aside.

She stretched out on her side atop her sleeping bag, propping her head in her hand. "What's your greatest fear?"

"Failure. I hate being called a fuckup."

"What's your proudest accomplishment?"

"So far? Brown Eyed Girl. But I think what we do together will top it."

"Same." She smiled. "Okay, last question. You go."

"What's your biggest regret?" I asked her quietly.

"I'm not sure I have one, as an adult. I suppose I regret being such a terrible teenager to my parents, but we have a good relationship now. They'll probably make me pay for it someday by moving in with me and making me take care of them when they're old and cranky all the time."

I laughed. "Probably."

"What about you?" She met my eyes. "What's your biggest regret?"

Raindrops thrummed steadily on the tent, and thunder continued to roll softly overhead. I inhaled and caught the scent of something she must have put on her skin—it was summery and sweet, and it mingled with the smell of the rain, which I'd always loved. I tucked her hair behind her ear. "Running away from you."

"Oliver." She closed her eyes. "Don't. You said you wouldn't."

"I might have lied."

She sighed. "This is why I can't trust you."

"Okay, it wasn't a lie exactly, but I might have … overestimated my ability to resist you. And I meant what I said." I brushed a thumb across her cheek. "I was a complete idiot to leave when I did, the way I did. And I've always regretted it."

"I don't believe you." Her lower lip trembled.

"Give me another chance, Chloe. I'm not that guy anymore."

She lifted her chin. "Prove it."

Fifteen

Chloe

NOW

Oliver looked confused. "Huh?"

"Prove it," I challenged. "Prove to me that you're not the same guy you were before."

"How?"

I pushed his hand away. "By keeping your promise not to lay a finger on me."

"But ... can't we think of another way?" He looked longingly at my bare legs.

"Nope." To reinforce my stance, I opened up my sleeping bag and got in it. "If you mean what you say, and you really do want another chance with me, you'll have no problem keeping your hands to yourself on *your* side of the tent. If you just want to get laid tonight and you're looking for an uncomplicated vagina, you'll have to seek it elsewhere."

"Because your vagina is complicated?"

I raised my chin. "It's *very* complicated."

"Fine." Sighing heavily, he reached over and turned

down the light, removed his T-shirt, then flopped onto his back, hands behind his head. "Goodnight."

"Goodnight." I turned onto my side, facing away from him, trying to hide a smile in the hoodie I was using as a pillow. I was *positive* he would be crawling over to me within minutes, proving me right.

Then, and *only then*, would I give in.

So I stayed awake and waited.

And waited.

And waited.

The thunder moved on, the rain eased to a drizzle, the crickets chirped louder … but Oliver stayed on his side of the tent.

Damn you, Oliver. I know you want me.

I sighed loudly, just to remind him I was there and let him know I wasn't asleep.

Nothing.

After another minute, I rolled onto my back and took my legs out of my sleeping bag.

Nothing.

I rolled onto my side, facing him, and peeked. He was in the exact same position he'd been in before. Eyes closed. His bare chest was visible, and it made my pelvic muscles contract.

I sighed again. Even louder.

"Can't sleep?" he asked, not moving a muscle. He had such a great profile.

"I guess not."

"How come? Too dark?"

"No."

"Too hot?"

"No."

"Too cold?"

"No."

"Then what is it? There must be something keeping you awake."

Out of patience, I sat up. "I changed my mind."

"Oh? About what?"

"About tonight." I leaned toward him and whispered coyly, "You can lay a finger on me."

"Nah, I better not." He still hadn't even opened his eyes.

Indignant, I straightened up. "What? Why not?"

"Because you were right. If I'm really going to prove myself and earn your trust, I need to keep my promises."

I sat there open-mouthed, trying to decide if I was impressed or offended.

"Plus, I'm sort of scared of your complicated vagina," he went on, a smile creeping onto his face. "I've never seen one of those before. I might not know what to do with it."

"Forget it," I snapped, flopping onto my side, facing away from him again. "Goodnight."

It wasn't even three seconds later that I felt his body pressing up behind mine and his hand sliding up my thigh. "I'm only fucking with you," he whispered, his lips against my ear. "I know exactly what to do with it."

"Get off me," I told him. "I don't want to play your little cat and mouse games."

"Come on, you love the games. You started this one."

"All you do is aggravate me."

"I know," he said, slipping his hand between my legs. "And right now I want to aggravate you *so hard*."

"I'm not in the mood."

"Liar." His fingers had edged past my underwear and easily slid inside me.

The hard length of his erection pressed at my tailbone, and I arched back against him. He buried his face in my neck, kissing my throat as his fingers worked magic between my legs. "I wish I didn't want you this way," I whispered. "You're nothing but trouble."

"You love trouble," he reminded me.

I rolled onto my back and slid a hand inside his shorts, sheathing his hot, hard cock with my fist. "Fuck you."

In an instant his mouth was on mine as he thrust through my fingers and I moved my hips against his hand. We were greedy and impatient, as if we wanted to make up for lost time. Barely breaking the kiss, we yanked at shorts and underwear and tugged off shirts, our skin growing sweaty, our breathing labored. In no time at all, he was poised above me, my legs wrapped around him.

"Is it okay?" he asked, teasing me with the tip of his cock.

"It's okay," I panted, my body unwilling to wait for my mind to stop and think this through.

Then he was easing inside, and I didn't care about anything but how good it felt to have Oliver moving over me, filling me up, rocking into my body harder and deeper every time. I raked my nails down his back and grabbed his ass, pulling him tighter against me. I moaned and sighed and cursed, hating myself for wanting him so badly, for letting him do this to me again, for knowing exactly how to make me come.

But I loved him for it too—loved the way he liked it a little rough, loved it when he got to his knees and yanked my hips onto his thighs, loved it when he rubbed his thumb over my clit while he drove his cock into me again and again and again. He groaned and growled and swore through clenched teeth. He told me he was going to come, and at the last second, he grabbed me beneath the arms and pulled me onto his lap, bringing me with him over the edge as I rode out the orgasm on his thick, throbbing cock.

"Jesus," I gasped, clinging to Oliver just to stay upright.

"That wasn't complicated at all." He was out of breath too.

"No," I agreed. "It wasn't. But we've complicated our business relationship significantly."

"We made it better, I'd say."

I leaned back to look him in the eyes, my arms still looped around his neck. "What are we going to do?"

"About what?"

"About *us*." Sighing, I took in his messy hair and handsome face, complete with the tiny scar on his chin he'd gotten when we jumped off the barn roof. "I'm scared we're going to ruin everything."

"Why?"

"Because that's what we do. That's the pattern, Oliver! We get close to something good, and then we blow it up. We rush it. I'm not blaming you entirely, I do it too."

"We're not doing that now," he insisted. "We were too young before. I wasn't ready." He tipped his forehead to mine. "But I feel something for you. No matter how much time passes, or how long I go without seeing you, it never goes away. The moment I'm with you again, it hits me"—he put a hand on his bare chest—"right here."

A strange fear was threatening to choke me. "Oliver. No."

"Feel this." He grabbed my hand and put it over his heart, which I felt thumping hard and fast beneath my palm.

My throat constricted. "That's from the sex."

"That's from you."

"And what's so different this time, huh?" I pulled my hand away. "How do I know this isn't another Chicago, where everything seems real and perfect, but by the time the sun comes up, you've changed your mind? I know you."

"And I know *you*. If you didn't feel something for me, if you didn't think what we have is too good to ignore, you'd have stayed on your side of the tent."

"Damn you and this tent." Sniffing again, I crossed my arms over my chest.

"This isn't Chicago, Chloe," he said quietly, taking my head in his hands. "I know I fucked that up. I know you're scared. I know you have no reason to believe me when I tell you things will be different now, but all I can do is ask you for one more chance. We could be so good together, Chloe."

"Oh, God." I closed my eyes and he kissed me again, soft and sweet. "I've spent so many nights cursing you for what you did. You made me feel worthless and foolish and angry. You made me hate you."

"I know. I hated myself."

I looked at him again, swallowed against the lump in my throat. "But I still missed you. I still wanted you."

His lips tipped up. "So you'll give me another chance?"

I nodded. "But you have to promise me something."

"Anything."

"No games. No bullshit. You have to be honest with me."

"I will."

I looked him right in the eye and stripped my soul bare. "I was prepared to give you everything seven years ago. And you broke my heart."

He nodded slowly, accepting the truth.

"But you've always had a piece of it," I whispered as my throat closed up again.

"I'm never giving it back." He crushed his lips to mine and gently tipped me backward, and we lay skin to skin, making out and whispering in the dark like the teenagers we used to be. Eventually, we slid inside his sleeping bag and held each other as we drifted off to sleep, my head on his chest.

When I woke up the next morning, I was alone in the tent. For a moment, I panicked—*he left me again.* Then I noticed all his stuff was still there and figured he must have gone to the bathroom or something. But when he didn't return after a couple minutes, I threw on the first clothing I could find, stuck my flip-flops on my feet, and went outside.

The morning air was crisp and cool, the woods damp, and I went back into the tent to grab my sweatshirt before heading down to the beach. Something told me that's where Oliver would be.

I saw him as soon as I stepped out from the trees and onto the bluff. He was sitting in the sand, facing the water with his arms draped over his knees. Zipping up my sweatshirt, against the slight chill, I made my way down the dune.

"Morning," I said, dropping onto my knees in the sand next to him.

"Hey. What are you doing up so early?" His hair was sticking out in every direction, and he quickly tried to fix it.

I put my hands in it, messing it up again. "Don't. I like it messy. It's cute."

He grinned and pulled me in front of him, settling me

between his legs, his arms wrapped around my shoulders. "Sleep okay?"

"I guess. Camping is fun, but I'm not gonna lie, I prefer a nice hotel."

He kissed my shoulder. "Same."

I hooked my hands over his forearms. "Did you sleep okay?"

"Okay enough."

"How long have you been down here?"

"Not too long." He paused. "I was a little restless this morning. Thinking about a lot of things. I didn't want to wake you."

We were silent for a couple minutes, watching the waves roll in. "When I woke up and noticed you were gone, I got a little nervous," I said.

"Did you think I'd abandoned you in the woods?"

"For a moment."

He pressed his lips to the side of my head. "You don't have to worry about that anymore."

I squeezed his arms. "So what will we do today?"

"I was thinking about that. I thought maybe we'd hike around the east side of the island on our way back to the docks to grab the ferry."

"Sounds good."

"And then," he went on, "I think we deserve a little celebration time. Alone."

I leaned to one side and looked back at him over my shoulder. "Oh yeah?"

"Yeah. When we get back to the mainland, I'm going to call my mom and tell her we'll be one more night. Then I'm going to make reservations for us to stay somewhere a little less rustic."

My pulse raced a little. "Really?"

"Yes. Is that okay?"

"Sure. Will your mom be upset?"

"I don't care." He kissed my temple. "I just got you all to myself, and I'm a selfish bastard. I don't want to share."

"What about your grandmother's birthday?"

"She'll still be ninety when we get there."

I laughed. "Our families are going to flip out about this. Our mothers are going to gloat."

"I don't care. If you're happy, I'm happy. Nothing else matters."

"I'm happy." I tipped my head back and rested it on his chest.

We ate some breakfast, packed up our campsite, and hiked around the east side of the island, reaching the docks before noon. We held hands almost the entire time. On the ferry ride, I rested my head on his shoulder and he kept a hand on my leg. When we got back to his car, he opened the passenger door for me and turned on the air conditioning before packing up the trunk with all our gear.

While he did that, I glanced in the visor mirror, cringing at my frizzy hat hair, sunburned nose, and sweaty face. I needed a shower, a blow dryer, and some serious time in the shade.

A hotel room would do nicely.

We grabbed lunch in Leland, and while we sat at the table, Oliver reserved a room at an inn not far from Sleeping Bear Dunes, where we'd once gone as kids together. Then he called his mother.

"Hey, Mom. Just wanted to let you know Chloe and I are going to be one more night." He paused, holding the phone tighter to his ear. Then he glanced at me. "Yes. She's right here." Another pause. "Yes. I'll tell her."

Tell me what? I wondered. And why was he looking a little nervous?

"No! You can talk to her later." His tone was vehement.

Talk to me? Why on earth would his mother want to talk to me right now?

Then he rolled his eyes. "Same here, Mom. I know. We're looking forward to seeing you too. It's only one extra night."

I sipped my iced tea, laughing when he made a jabbering gesturing with his hand, as if his mother wouldn't stop talking. My mom was the exact same way.

"Okay, Mom, gotta go. Chloe's waiting for me, and you don't want to miss the tournament. Yep, see you tomorrow. Bye."

"Tournament?" I asked. "What kind of tournament?"

"Croquet. It's very serious in my family."

"Oh my God. That is so Pemberton." I laughed and set my iced tea on the table. "I'm going to use the restroom real quick. Be right back."

"Take your time."

I grabbed my purse and headed into the women's room, thankful for a real toilet and sink. After I washed my hands, I quickly dug in my purse for my pack of birth control pills. Given what had gone on last night and what would likely continue for the foreseeable future, I'd have to be vigilant about them. Oliver and I needed a chance to make it work for the right reasons, *real* reasons—by choice, not because we were out to win a bet or prove something or impress each other. And definitely not because of a missed pill. But as I swallowed one, I found myself wondering if there would ever come a time when I wouldn't worry about it so much.

Before I went back to the table, I decided to call April real quick. She picked up right away.

"You're alive," she said by way of hello. "Are you in a trunk?"

I laughed. "No. I'm in a restaurant bathroom in Leland, but last night we were camping on South Manitou."

She gasped. "Alone?"

"Alone in a *tent*."

Silence. "Did you?"

"We did." I cringed, feeling like I had to defend myself. "But it's not what you think."

"You said you weren't going to let him charm you."

"I know, I know." I bit my lip. "But he seems different this time."

"What about Chicago?"

"We talked about it. He apologized."

"What was his excuse?"

"That he was young and immature. Not ready to face his feelings."

April sighed. "He still could have called you."

I stared at some graffiti on the wall. "You think I'm being stupid?"

"No, of course not. I just know you tend to rush into things. But I also know that you two have a lot of history."

"We do. And there's just something about him I can't resist, even though I know I should. He … *gets* to me. I don't know how to explain it."

"It's good chemistry. You don't have to explain it. Just take it slow."

"I will." A woman and her little girl came into the bathroom. "Listen, I have to go. We're spending the night around here tonight and then heading to Harbor Springs tomorrow to see his family."

She laughed. "That's not exactly taking it slow."

I laughed too as I went out the door. "I know. But it feels good right now, and we're so excited about the distillery plans. I have tons to tell you when I get back."

"I can't wait to hear them." She hesitated. "I like Oliver, Chloe. I really do. And if he can help you see your distillery dream come true, I'll like him even more."

"I feel like there's a but coming."

"But as your big sister," she went on, "I just want you to be cautious. You have a tendency to leap before you look."

"I know." I looked up and saw Oliver smile at me, and my stomach went weightless. "I'll be careful."

But as I dropped my phone back into my purse and made my way back to the table, I couldn't help feeling like my grip on caution was getting weaker with every beat of my heart.

Was I crazy to think this time it was real?

Sixteen

Chloe

THEN

"CHLOE?"

I was in line for the bar at a hospital charity gala when I heard my name. The deep voice had come from over my left shoulder, and I glanced behind me. "Oliver?"

He grinned. "I thought that was you."

"From the back? How did you even recognize me?"

"The tattoo."

"Oh. Duh." I'd forgotten I was wearing a dress with a low back, and my hair was up too, making the line of script across my shoulder blades plainly visible.

"How are you?" He leaned in to kiss my cheek, and I let him. He looked good, of course, perfectly turned out in a charcoal suit and striped tie.

"Fine."

He grinned. "I'm fine too."

"I didn't ask."

He tipped up his drink. "You look great."

"Thanks. So do you." I glanced at his legs. "Decided to wear pants to this occasion, huh?"

He laughed. "Indeed I did."

I looked straight ahead again, wishing my skin didn't feel quite so warm. It was like he radiated some kind of thermal energy my body was conditioned to respond to. I'd been perfectly cool a moment ago.

"I take it you're still angry about what happened at Hughie's party," he said.

I shrugged.

"Come on, there are bigger crimes in the world than giving someone an orgasm."

"Shush!" I glanced around, making sure no one heard. "That wasn't the reason I got mad, and you know it."

"What was the reason again?"

We moved forward in line. "Your moral repugnance."

"Oh, good. I thought it was something serious."

I gave him a dirty look. "What are you doing here?"

"In Chicago or at this event?"

"Both."

"I'm in town visiting a friend. His mom is on the board at the hospital. What about you?"

"I came with my roommate. She works for the hospital foundation. And my company does their PR."

"Ah." He swirled the honey-colored liquid in his glass. "I've reached out a few times over the last year or so. Sent you a few texts."

"Oh really? I didn't get them," I said. "Maybe you have the wrong number."

He smiled, because he knew I was lying.

A moment later, we reached the front of the line, and Oliver asked me what I'd like.

"Vodka and soda with a lime, please," I said to the bartender. I'd be damned if I'd let him order for me.

The bartender nodded and looked at Oliver. "And for you?"

"Nothing for me, thanks."

While my drink was being poured, I put a dollar in the tip jar and checked my phone. It was only nine, and I was already bored stiff at this event. I wasn't really a gala sort of person, and while I liked supporting a good cause with my work, standing around in a fancy dress and high heels making small talk with stiff rich people got old fast. My roommate had disappeared an hour ago with a recently divorced surgeon she'd been crushing on, and I had a feeling they'd gotten a room upstairs. But I didn't want to leave without hearing from her.

The bartender returned with my cocktail, and Oliver reached for it. "I'll carry it for you," he said. "Where are you sitting?"

"Where's your date?" I asked, moving away from the bar. "Isn't she missing you by now?"

He followed me. "I came with a guy friend, and while he *is* gay, I'm pretty sure I'm not his type."

"Oh." I looked over toward my table, which I wasn't particularly excited about returning to. "I was sitting over there, but …"

"You don't want to sit?"

"Not really." I took my drink from his hand and sipped, making a face. "Ew. This is totally watered-down, and I think he put tonic in it, not soda."

"Want me to get another one for you?"

I sighed and shook my head. "Don't worry about it."

"Listen. Why don't we go upstairs to the hotel bar and get a real drink?"

"I don't know. I'm kind of tired." I checked my phone, and sure enough, the message from my roommate said *Staying here tonight!!!*

"Come on, Dimples," Oliver prodded. "I'm buying, and we can catch up. We haven't seen each other in, what, two years?"

"Three," I said, narrowing my eyes at him, because he knew *exactly* when it was. "Hughie's party, remember?

"I remember." He finished his drink, his eyes dancing over the rim of his glass. "So what do you say? One drink for old times' sake? I promise I'm not carrying any rubber snakes, nor will I dare you to jump off the roof."

"Your promises mean nothing to me, Oliver Pemberton. Because you never keep them." I frowned at my crappy cocktail. "But I would like a good drink before I go."

He laughed, taking the full glass from my hand and setting it alongside his empty one on a nearby service tray. "You got it. Let's go. One drink, and then I'll get you an Uber."

I sighed. "Fine."

We made our way toward the hotel elevators, and I stumbled slightly on the long hem of my dress. Oliver immediately took my arm. "You okay?"

"Yeah. I borrowed this dress, so it's not a perfect fit. My roommate is taller than I am."

"Who isn't?"

I glared at him but let him keep my arm in his grasp. I didn't necessarily like him touching me—my body always reacted to his touch—but I didn't want to face-plant, either.

Side by side, we rode the elevator in silence, and when the doors opened, Oliver led me through them. A woman waiting to board the elevator smiled at us. "What a beautiful couple," she said.

"Thank you," Oliver replied.

"But we're not a couple," I added, taking my arm back. I lifted up the hem of my dress as we walked across the lobby to the bar.

It was crowded, and I didn't see anywhere to sit except for a few tables with Reserved signs on them. "Should we go somewhere else?" I asked.

"No. Give me one minute." Oliver went over to the host, took some cash from his wallet and slipped it to him. A moment later, he was back.

"We can sit anywhere we'd like," he said confidently.

I was annoyed and relieved at the same time. My feet were killing me. "How about over there?" I pointed to a small corner booth with a round table.

"Perfect." He took my arm again and guided me toward the spot.

We slid into the booth, and I immediately took off my shoes. A waiter came over and asked what we'd like, and Oliver looked at me. "What sounds good? Vodka?"

"What are you having?"

"Probably scotch."

"I'll do that too."

He discussed the selection with the server and made his choice. When we were alone again, he leaned back and put his arm along the back of the seat, just above my shoulders.

I glanced at it, then at him. "Really?"

"Is it bothering you?"

Grumbling, I shifted on the plush bench seat. "It's fine. As long as you understand things are not getting romantic between us tonight."

"When have things ever been *romantic* between us?"

"You know what I mean. Nothing is going to happen. I'm having one drink, and I'm going home."

Our eyes locked, and a slow smile crept onto his lips. "Okay."

Needless to say, something happened.

I'm not even sure how.

One drink turned into two. Then three. We caught up. Laughed about old times. Asked about family. We shared stories, looked at pictures on each other's phones, discussed the scotch.

When our glasses were empty, Oliver paid the bill and we walked out to the elevators. I was pleasantly tipsy by then, but I still caught him hitting the up arrow.

"Hey," I said. "I have to get my coat. The ballroom is on the lower level."

"I know." The doors opened, and he stepped inside. The car was empty. "But my room is upstairs."

I didn't move. He held his finger on the button, keeping the doors open, and met my eyes. The look on his face dared me to get on. Go up to his room. Get naked.

I wished he didn't look so fucking good in that suit.

"One," he said.

I held my ground, but felt it cracking under my feet.

"Two."

I clenched my stomach muscles, remembering how big he was, how he used his mouth, how quickly he made me come.

"Three." He took his hand off the button. "Goodnight, Chloe."

The doors began to close.

My hand shot out.

The doors opened again and I stepped through them, breathing hard. "You're fucking impossible," I told him.

"And you're fucking predictable." He lowered his voice.

"But I've been waiting for this a long time."

The doors closed behind me, and we went at each other like wolves.

Fueled by pent-up lust and scotch, we stumbled into Oliver's room and tore at each other's clothes. It was hot and rough and a little bit violent, as if we were furious we hadn't been able to keep our hands to ourselves and wanted to take it out on one another's bodies. We pushed and pulled and growled and grasped. We called each other names and cursed viciously. We knocked over a lamp and ripped Oliver's shirt.

When we finally exploded together, Oliver had me up against the door, and if our yelling didn't wake the entire floor, then the pounding must have. I'd have bruises for days.

Afterward, we collapsed on the bed, naked and sweaty and exhausted.

"Oh my God," I said. "I can't believe we did that."

"I know. Me either."

"I think I pulled a muscle."

"I think you bit me. Am I bleeding?"

I laughed. "No, but I hope you're not seeing anyone. If you are, she's going to wonder about all those scratches on your back."

"I'm not seeing anyone." He paused. "Are you?"

"No."

Neither of us moved for several minutes. When I caught myself falling asleep, I sat up. "I should go."

"Why? Just stay here."

I looked down at him. "You want me to stay?"

"Yeah." He opened his eyes. In the low light, they almost looked black instead of blue. "Spend the night with me."

I waited for it—the dirty joke, the excuse, the subtle dig—the reason he'd toss out for asking me to stay. It couldn't just be that he wanted me here.

But he didn't say anything more. He just reached out and covered my hand with his.

I looked at our hands for a moment, and a thousand memories came rushing back. Some good, some bad, but all us. I felt close to him, and I didn't want to leave. "Okay. I'll stay."

"Good." He took off his watch and put it on the nightstand.

"What should we do today?" Oliver traced the letters of my tattoo with his finger. "Museum? Aquarium? Stroll down Michigan Avenue?"

I was on my stomach, arms folded beneath my pillow. "What day is it?"

He laughed. "Saturday. Do you have to be somewhere?"

I tried to think, but my brain, like my body, was complete mush. We'd spent the entire night alternating between mind-blowing sex and short, heavy naps. Neither of us had gotten enough sleep. "I can't remember."

"You don't work on Saturdays, do you?"

"No."

"Good. Spend the day with me."

"I have no clothes."

"Even better." He looked at the window. "It's raining anyway. We'll just stay in bed."

Smiling, I looked at his tousled hair and stubbled jaw. "How long are you in Chicago?"

"For the weekend."

"Do you have plans?"

"Yes. Fucking you ten different ways. Giving you lots of orgasms. Making you scream my name some more." He leaned down and kissed my shoulder. "Doesn't that sound fun?"

Of course it did. But I wasn't sure my body could take another day of it.

"I don't know, Oliver. I'm kind of sore." I tried to stretch and winced at the pain in my back muscles.

"I have been pretty rough on you, haven't I?" He sounded proud.

"Yes." I flipped onto my side and threw an arm and a leg over him. "But I like it."

He pinched my ass hard. "That's my girl."

During the next two days, Oliver only left the room twice—once to run down to the ballroom and get my coat and then to the lobby store to pick up a toothbrush for me, and the second time to buy more condoms.

I never left once all weekend.

We ate ridiculously expensive room service meals, drank a pricey bottle of bourbon, rehashed childhood memories, argued incessantly about everything under the sun, and had so much sex I didn't think I'd be able to walk out of there.

And somewhere in between all the eating and drinking and laughing and orgasms, the idea for Brown Eyed Girl was born.

"I just don't know what I want to do with my life," he'd said, taking another five-dollar mozzarella stick from the basket. "Now that I'm done with grad school, my parents want me to come home and work for Pemberton, but I don't want a desk job. I'm scared if I take it, they'll turn me into someone I have no interest in becoming. I'll wake up one day and discover I hate my life but it'll be too late to do anything about it. I'll have a boring job, an ex-wife who can't stand me, and two kids who blame me for fucking up their lives. Even the dog will hate me."

I giggled. "So don't take that job. Change course. Do something else."

"Like what?"

"I don't know. What do you love?"

He thought for a second. "Sex, sailboats, and whiskey."

"Well, I'm not sure how to make a living with the first two, but want to hear about an idea I've been kicking around that involves whiskey?"

"Yes." Stretching out on his side on the bed, wearing only a pair of jeans, he propped his head on his hands.

"I'm moving back to Cloverleigh this fall to take over the marketing and PR, as well as manage the tasting rooms at the winery. And I've been thinking about starting a small batch distillery."

"That's so crazy. I've thought about that too," he said excitedly. "Ever since I took that trip to Scotland, it's been in my head."

"Really?"

"Yeah." He shook his head. "It's like we share brain waves or something."

I grinned. "We might."

"So when will you do it?"

"I'm not sure. Not right away—I've got more research to do, and I need to make sure I have the financial resources, but I'm excited about it."

"I've got financial resources. Let's do it together."

"What?" I stared at him.

"I just turned twenty-five and inherited a chunk of my trust. Let's do it together." He thought for a second. "But maybe we should locate it somewhere other than the farm. Cloverleigh gets a lot of wine people and families, but we'd want a different demographic—younger and hipper."

"You're thinking here? Chicago?"

"Not necessarily. What about Detroit? There are some distilleries doing well there already. We'd have to think of a way to stand out, but I bet we could do it."

I sat up. "Oliver, are you serious? You'd go into business with me?"

"Of course I would." He grinned at me. "Let's do it."

We stayed up half the night taking notes and researching things online and sketching ideas on hotel stationary. We figured we'd start with something simpler to make, like a vodka or gin, and then work our way into whiskey, which was more difficult and took more time. As the hours passed, we got more and more excited, convinced this was the best fucking idea in the world, we were geniuses, and everyone was going to say they knew us when. We might have been half drunk, or half crazy—probably both—but at that moment, the entire world belonged to us.

"Would you move to Detroit?" he asked, leaning back against the pillows, stretching his legs out in front of him. He wore only a pair of hunter green boxer briefs, and his bare chest bore faint red scratch marks.

"Fuck yes, I would." I sat cross-legged next to him in one

of his T-shirts, our pile of notes between us. "I'll start looking for PR jobs there right away, since our business won't turn a profit for a while."

"Don't worry about that. I'll make sure you have enough money so you don't have to work another job. The marketing is going to be critical for us. There's a lot of competition."

I stared at Oliver. "You're going to pay me a salary? Out of your trust?

"It's an investment. And you're worth it." He reached for me, pulling me onto his lap so that I straddled him. "I think you should quit your job on Monday and move up to Detroit."

I laughed. "You're insane!"

"Probably."

"I don't even have a place to live in Detroit."

"So stay with me until you find a place." He tucked my hair behind my ears. "Or as long as you want to."

"Oliver," I whispered, my heart beating madly. "What is this?"

"I don't know. I just know that I don't want it to end tomorrow when you walk out of here."

"I don't either."

We stared at each other for a moment, then he grabbed my head and crushed his lips to mine. "I know what we should call our company."

"What?" I asked breathlessly.

"Brown Eyed Girl."

"Like the song?"

"Like you."

The room was spinning, and I wasn't sure which way was up.

Within minutes, his underwear and my T-shirt were on the floor and he was sliding inside me again. It felt different this time. Less playful. More intense. We weren't fucking just for fun or because we were bored or because it felt good—we were doing it because we felt something for *each other*.

And when we said goodbye late Sunday night, we kissed deep and long and said we'd see each other soon.

The next morning, I gave my notice at work.

Two days later, I told my roommate I was moving out by the end of the month.

Three days later, I told my parents I wouldn't be moving home to work at Cloverleigh.

I thought it was a little strange that I hadn't heard from Oliver, but I never would have guessed why.

He was already gone.

Oliver

THEN

ALISON WAS SERIOUSLY GETTING ON MY NERVES.

"My shoes are going to be ruined."

"It's snowing, Alison. What do you want me to do? I can't get you any closer to the door than valet."

She huffed, but remained silent as I pulled forward. We were attending the Cloverleigh Christmas party at the request of my parents. Hughie and Lisa were here too, showing off their brand new baby. I really hadn't wanted to come, but my mother had guilt-tripped me. My mood was anything but festive.

"You knew what the weather was like when you got dressed," I said irritably, putting my SUV in park. "This is northern Michigan. We get snow in December."

"I know, Oliver. I'm from Kenilworth, not Kenya."

Leaving the keys in the ignition, I nodded tersely at the valet and went around to the passenger side. A second attendant had opened Alison's door, and I helped her out. "They put salt down, so it shouldn't be too icy."

"Great," she said sarcastically, eyeing the walk leading to the front door of the inn. "That's even worse for my shoes."

Jesus fucking Christ, I thought, carefully leading her toward the door. *It's a ten-foot walk. Do you want me to carry you?*

"I don't even know why we're here. Who are these people again?" she asked for the hundredth time.

I clenched my jaw. "John and Daphne Sawyer. They own Cloverleigh Farms."

"And how do you know them?"

"Daphne and my mother grew up together. They've been best friends for fifty years." I held the door open for her. "Our families have always been close."

"Do they have kids?"

"Five daughters. Sylvia, April, Meg, Frannie, and Chloe."

I hadn't spoken to Chloe since she left my Chicago hotel room four years ago, and saying her name out loud made me feel a little strange. Would it be awkward seeing her tonight? Was she still mad? I'd tried reaching out after I'd come home from Europe, but judging from the expletive-heavy response to my *hey, how are you* text message, she was still pretty pissed. I'd never seen so many F-bombs in one sentence.

"Are any of the daughters married?" Alison glanced at the engagement ring on her finger as I pulled open the heavy front door.

"Only Sylvia, the oldest." I could tell by the look on her face she felt some kind of victory in her pre-marital status, as if the diamond on her finger made her a better person.

Once inside, we checked our coats and greeted the Sawyers, who stood chatting with my parents by the fireplace. I introduced them to Alison, and felt bad when

Aunt Daphne tried to hug her and my fiancée remained stiff. Alison wasn't really a hugger. It didn't bother me, since I wasn't particularly inclined to be affectionate with her. Alison was perfect on paper, nearly a carbon copy of Hughie's wife, in fact, but I wasn't in love with her. The *idea* of her made my family happy—it reassured them that I was finally settling down—but mostly she drove me nuts.

April Sawyer came over to say hello, and I kissed her cheek. "Good to see you, April. This is Alison."

"His fiancée," Alison informed her, holding out a pale, manicured hand.

"Of course." April smiled warmly at her and glanced at the ring. "So nice to meet you, and congratulations on your engagement."

"Thank you. We're *very* happy." Alison gave me a look like I was a dog who hadn't performed a trick when prompted.

"I need a drink," I said. "Can I get either of you anything?"

"I'm fine," April said. "But order anything you like at the bar."

"I'll take a glass of wine." Alison looked around at the guests, mostly family, close friends, and employees of Cloverleigh. I could totally imagine her sizing everyone up, judging them by what they wore. Things like labels mattered to her.

"We have great wine here," said April. "Oliver, take her into the bar and check out the new renovations."

"I'll do that, thanks." I took Alison's arm, mostly because she expected me to, and led her into the restaurant. The bar was over to one side, and I immediately spotted Chloe standing at it with friends. She held a drink in her hand, and she was laughing at something someone had said, her face all lit up.

She was even more beautiful than I remembered, and I remembered her a lot.

It wasn't even on purpose. Thinking about Chloe made me feel shitty—I knew I shouldn't have done what I did, and I had no good excuse. I'd tried, over the last few years, to pinpoint exactly what it was that made me abandon her that way, and I hadn't come up with one good reason except … I was an immature jackass and not ready to take anything seriously. But she'd always known that about me, hadn't she? And really, we hadn't made any promises to each other. We'd just tossed around some ideas. She couldn't hold it against me forever.

Avoiding her for now, I steered Alison toward the opposite end of the bar, barely noticing the renovations April had mentioned.

"What's wrong?" Alison asked. "You look like you've seen a ghost."

"Nothing." I cleared my throat and faced the bartender. "What kind of red wine do you have?"

He listed some of Cloverleigh's varietals.

"Are they all from Michigan?" Alison asked, turning up her nose.

It made me angry, but rather than defend the merits of Michigan wine, I bit my tongue. While the bartender went through additional choices, I snuck a glance at Chloe over Alison's shoulder. She was still smiling, and her dimples made my pulse quicken. Goddammit, why wasn't it *me* making her laugh?

"Oliver?"

I looked at Alison and blinked. "What?"

"What do you want to drink?" She pointed her nose at the bartender, who had clearly been waiting for my order.

"Oh, sorry." Scanning the shelves behind the bar—I wasn't surprised to note they held no Brown Eyed Girl spirits—I ordered a Kentucky bourbon and told myself not to look at Chloe again.

But the moment Alison started glancing around and listing all the reasons why she wouldn't hold a wedding here—too small, too dark, too rustic—I found it impossible not to let my eyes wander over her shoulder again.

This time, Chloe spotted me. I knew the moment it happened, because the grin slid right off her face, and her entire demeanor changed. Her posture went stiff. Her eyes narrowed. She pressed her lips together. Tension hummed in the air between us, and beneath my suit, gooseflesh prickled over my skin.

She looked back at the person she'd been talking to, and I attempted to refocus on Alison. But even after our drinks arrived and I took a few big swallows to steady my nerves, I could not keep my eyes where they were supposed to be.

Alison finally complained. "You're not listening to a word I'm saying. And who on earth do you keep looking at behind me?"

"No one."

She glanced over her shoulder, and I swear to God she used some kind of black-magic, sixth-sense bullshit to zero right in on Chloe. "Who is she?"

I played dumb. "Who?"

She focused on me with laser-like intensity. "That girl you were looking at with the dark hair in the short black dress."

I pretended to look for the woman in question. "You mean Chloe?"

"I don't know, Oliver," she snapped. "*Do* I mean Chloe?"

"I think so. She's one of the Sawyer sisters."

She looked over her shoulder again, and unfortunately it was at the exact same second Chloe's eyes shifted to me once more.

A tense moment followed, then Chloe gave me the finger.

I'd have laughed if I wasn't so on edge.

Alison, who was too cool to make a scene, turned to face me again. "What's that all about?"

I swallowed some bourbon. "It's nothing. Childhood grudge—she and I used to be really competitive. I beat her at everything."

"And now she flips you the bird at parties." Alison took another sip of wine. "Classy."

"She's just—" I stopped, unsure how to describe Chloe. It wasn't that she lacked class, she simply didn't tolerate bullshit. You had to respect her for it. "We just have a certain kind of history is all."

"Did you sleep with her?"

"What? No." I ran a hand over my hair. "Of course not. We've known each other since birth."

"You better not be lying to me, Oliver."

"I'm not," I lied.

"Either way, she's not coming to the wedding." She said it like that was the worst punishment she could mete out to someone.

For fuck's sake, I wish *I* didn't have to come to the wedding. The thought of spending the rest of my life with Alison was stifling, and that ring had set me back a fuck ton.

It wasn't even the original one I'd presented—when we'd taken it to get fitted, she'd requested a *bigger* rock.

Alison set her empty wine glass on the bar. "Could you order me another glass, please? And bring it out to the other room with the fireplace? I'm going to find Lisa and Hughie."

"Fine."

Alison walked out of the bar with her nose in the air, barely giving Chloe another glance. Part of me wanted to run and hide. But I knew if I didn't face her now, I'd never be able to look her in the eye. Fuck that.

Straightening my tie, I puffed up my chest and walked her way. "Chloe."

"Oliver." She didn't introduce me to her friends.

"Can I speak to you for a minute?"

"Why?"

"To catch up. We haven't seen each other in a while."

"Whose fault is that?"

I frowned. "Could we please have this conversation in private?"

"I never want to have another conversation with you again, in private or anywhere else."

My temper flared at being put in my place in front of strangers. "You're being a little juvenile about this, aren't you?"

She coughed, putting a hand on her chest. "*I'm* being juvenile?"

This argument was going to embarrass us both, so I grabbed her by the arm and dragged her over to a dark corner of the restaurant that wasn't being used.

"Let go of me." She shook me off. "Asshole."

"Fine. I'm an asshole. But you can at least hear me out."

She crossed her arms. "You have ten seconds."

"I take it you're mad about Brown Eyed Girl."

"*Yes*, I'm mad about Brown Eyed Girl." Her eyes narrowed and glittered in the dark. "That was my idea and you stole it."

"Chloe, be fair. I didn't steal the idea—we both wanted to start a distillery, and we talked about doing it together. But when I got home from Europe, you weren't even speaking to me."

"With good reason."

"I tried texting you. You told me to fuck off."

"That's because your text said *hey, how are you*! Not *I'm sorry* or *please forgive me* or any of the things you should have told me."

"I was going to get around to that. You didn't give me a chance!"

She shook her head. "How could you have taken off on me like that?"

"I don't know," I said lamely. "It was an asshole move. I admit it."

"Gee, that's big of you."

"Look, that weekend was crazy. Neither of us was thinking straight."

"At least we agree on *something*. I don't know what possessed me to believe you were serious." She put a hand on her chest. "I quit my job, Oliver. I was ready to move to Detroit. I followed through, and you fucking blew me off."

"Okay, but it's been four years, Chloe. When are you going to get over it?"

"When I can look at your face and not want to hit you."

"You want to hit me? Do it. I dare you."

We faced off, and I could see the fury in her eyes. Still, I was as shocked as I'd ever been when I felt her palm strike my cheek—*hard*.

Then she gasped, clasping her hand to her chest, as if it had stunned her too.

I moved my jaw right and left, satisfied she hadn't done any real damage, although it stung like a motherfucker. "Feel better?"

"A little." She paused. "Did it hurt?"

"Nah. You hit like a girl."

"Can I try it again?" she asked through clenched teeth.

"No." In case she had any ideas, I backed up. "So are we good now?"

"You and I are never going to be good, Oliver. But have a nice life. I'm sure you'll be very happy with Elsa."

"You mean Alison?"

She shrugged. "I don't know her name. She just looks like the type to set off an eternal winter."

I grimaced. "Look, I don't want to be enemies, Chloe. We go back a long way."

She exhaled. "Fine. We're not enemies. But we're not friends either. And your ten seconds are up." She brushed by me and returned to her friends.

I went to the bar and got another round for Alison and me, then joined her in the lobby where she was talking to my brother and his wife. Chloe and I didn't speak again.

She did get the last word, though.

On the ride home, during which Alison was being even frostier than usual, she snipped, "Tell me the truth. Did you ever have sex with that Chloe girl or not?"

"Why?"

"Because she said something weird to me. Either she's seen you naked or she hates you."

"What did she say?"

"Just now, in the lobby bathroom before we left, I

came out of the stall to wash my hands and she was putting lipstick on in the mirror. She congratulated me on our engagement."

"That doesn't sound—"

"*Then* she said, 'Lucky you. That great big dick in your bed for the rest of your life.'"

I burst out laughing.

"So was she calling you a name or referring to part of your anatomy?" Alison demanded. "Tell me now."

"Both," I said, even though I knew she was going to give me hell for lying to her.

But I couldn't help it. Only Chloe would say something like that. I realized then how much I missed her in my life.

Would she ever forgive me?

Eighteen

Oliver

NOW

THE SMILE ON CHLOE'S FACE AS SHE WALKED BACK TO THE table was one I had only seen once before, in a hotel room in Chicago after I'd asked her to move in with me. It was sweet. Genuine. Tender.

And it made me feel like shit.

She'd opened herself up to trusting me, and I was still keeping the truth from her. I had to tell her the thing I didn't want to tell her, but I couldn't bring myself to do it yet. There would be fireworks for sure. Accusations. Rage. That adoring smile would slide right off her face, and I might never see it again.

I'd messed things up with Chloe before, and it had taken me years to get this second chance. I wasn't an idiot—there wouldn't be a third, so I had to get this right.

Should I tell her now?

Part of me knew it would be the best strategy, especially since my mother would soon be involved. I love her, but she is the worst secret-keeper ever. She just gets so excited and can't help herself. I could totally imagine my mother saying things to Chloe that would tip her off as to what I had done. The lie I'd told. The plan I'd put in place.

It was all a means to an end, and I'd thought it would be worth it, but I was less and less certain Chloe would agree. This thing between us had me all messed up. How had I not anticipated it? What a fucking idiot I was.

"Hey," she said, sliding into the booth across from me. "Ready to go? I'm dying for a shower."

The thought of her in the shower was a welcome distraction. "What a coincidence," I said, taking an uneaten fry from her plate and sticking it in my mouth. "I am too."

We drove to the inn, checked in, and brought our bags to the room. It felt good to open a hotel room door and watch Chloe walk in ahead of me. To carry her suitcase for her. To watch her set her purse on the desk and look at the king-sized bed, knowing we'd sleep in it together tonight.

Among other things.

"This is weird, isn't it?" she asked as the door slammed shut behind me.

"What is?"

"Us checking into a hotel room together."

I laughed. "I was just thinking how cool it was."

She grinned ruefully. "If anyone would have told me yesterday …"

"I know." I took my wallet and phone from my pocket and set them on the dresser. "When I was driving up on Sunday, I wasn't even sure I could get you to talk to me."

"I wasn't sure I was going to." She turned around and sat at the foot of the bed to untie her hiking boots. "You were pretty persuasive."

"I had to be." Dropping down next to her, I did the same.

"I had years of resentment to overcome. Those were some pretty big walls I had to tear down."

"Well, you smashed them to pieces, I'd say." She stared at the laces she'd just undone. "Congratulations."

"Hey." I knelt on the floor at her feet. "What's wrong?"

She took a breath. "I was just thinking how I spent years building up my defenses where you're concerned, and you destroyed them in one night. It's a little frightening, to be honest."

"You have nothing to be scared of, Chloe. I'll be honest. When I came here to ask you to partner up with me, it was strictly business. I was hoping we could be friends again, and partners going forward, but I had no idea *this* would happen."

"And what is *this*?" she asked. "What are we doing?"

"Well, first we're going to take a shower." I pulled off her boots. "Then maybe a little nap, since we didn't get much sleep last night." I tugged off her socks. "Then I thought maybe we could explore the dunes a little, have some dinner, take a walk. Or we can stay in our room all night, fuck like bunnies, and scheme to take over the world." Standing up, I took her by the hands and brought her to her feet. "I'm up for anything, as long as I'm with you."

She smiled. "Okay. I guess I just need to stop worrying. Can I have a five minute head start in the shower?"

"You …" I kissed her forehead. "Can have anything you want."

As she undressed and slipped into the bathroom, the smile was back on her face.

All I had to do was figure out how to keep it there.

"What book is this from again?" I traced the script tattooed on her back as the steam rose in hot clouds around us.

"It's not from a book, it's from a play, and I have told you that a million times." She gave me a dirty look over one shoulder.

I grinned. "Sorry. What play?"

"A Midsummer Night's Dream." She stood up taller and raised one fist. "O, when she is angry, she is keen and shrewd. She was a vixen when she went to school, and though she be but little, she is fierce."

I applauded her performance, and she turned around and curtsied. "Thank you. It's the only thing I remember from high school English."

I wrapped my arms around her. "It suits you. I like that whole vixen part."

"I liked that part too. It was the only character in a Shakespeare play I ever related to." She put her hands on my chest. "What was your favorite book in high school?"

"I don't remember anything from high school."

She rolled her eyes. "Come on. Not one academic memory? Nothing that left an impression on your young mind?"

I tilted my head and tried to think back. "Oh, wait. There is something I remember. Mackenzie Williams sat in front of me in American Lit, and she sometimes wore this really short skirt. So every now and then, I'd drop my pencil and—"

"Okay, enough." She closed her eyes. "That's not really what I meant, and I don't think I want to hear the end of that story. You can stop talking."

"Fine with me." I kissed the top of her head, inhaling the scent of her shampoo. She'd let me wash her hair, and then she'd washed mine. No one had ever done that for me before, and I couldn't believe how good it felt.

She'd let me soap her up too, and I got stupid hard running my hands all over her body and watching her rinse the lather from her skin. She'd done the same for me, and I loved the way her eyes widened at the sight of my erection.

I was still hard. And she was staring down at it again.

"Sorry. I've just never seen it in the daytime," she said, letting it slide through both hands.

"Don't apologize. Does that mean you're impressed?"

She nodded. "I have to admit I am. It's so *tall*."

"Thank you. But if you keep doing that with your hands, it's not going to last."

"Oh yeah?" A devilish gleam popped into her eye. "Like how fast could I make it happen?"

"Pretty fucking fast." I clenched my jaw, determined not to explode like a teenager.

"Do you think you could last five minutes?" She gripped me tighter, stroked a little faster.

"Uh ..." Fuck me, there was no way.

"I'll bet you can't." Laughing like the evil little vixen she was, she dropped to her knees. "I'll bet you lose control in three."

"Three?" I croaked, bracing one hand on the shower wall as she rubbed her lips all over my cock.

"Uh huh." She took the crown in her mouth and sucked. "Mm. Maybe even two. I can taste it already."

"Oh, Jesus." I wrapped my other hand around the shower curtain rod. "What are we betting?"

She paused. "Now let's see. How about this—if I can make you come in under five minutes, you make me CEO of Brown Eyed Girl. President, with a fifty-one percent stake."

She flicked the tip of my cock with her tongue. "Essentially, you work for me."

I fought for control. "And if I can hold out?"

"Then you get fifty-one percent."

I groaned. "What if I don't want to take the bet?"

She laughed and looked up at me, pure delight in her eyes. "Oh, you'll take the bet. I know you, Oliver Ford Pemberton. You can't resist."

Damn her. She knew me too well. "When does the clock start?"

"Do we agree on a gentleman's clock? Or do I have to set the alarm on my phone, like you did?"

"Fuck!" This was revenge. I could feel it. But I couldn't say no. "Fine. Gentleman's clock. Gentleman's clock. Just … don't stop."

She had both hands on my shaft and was licking the tip of my dick like an ice cream cone. She was making noises too—ridiculous, over-the-top noises that couldn't be real and yet *I fucking loved them*. I knew she was putting on a show for me, proving a point just to win the bet, but I didn't care.

Surely no Shakespearean actress was ever more magnificent in a performance. She moaned. She panted. She licked and sucked. She looked up at me with innocent wide brown eyes. She took me to the back of her throat. She slid a hand between her legs and touched herself as her lips glided up and down my cock over and over again.

As for me, I cursed. I seethed. I yanked on that curtain rod so hard I thought for sure it was going to come down. I battled for control, and I battled hard—if I lost this bet, I lost control of Brown Eyed Girl. It wasn't that I didn't trust Chloe, but once she knew the whole truth, she might not want it anyway.

Fuck, I couldn't think about that now. And I couldn't think about her mouth on my dick. Or how badly I wanted to come. Or how my body seemed to be moving without my permission, my hips jutting forward, jabbing my cock in deep and fast, fucking her mouth like I'd fantasized about so many times.

But no—no! I could hold out. I was strong. I was powerful. I was a *man*, and I was not going to go down without a fight.

Desperately, I tried to focus on other things. Unsexy things. Terrible, boring things.

Pemberton board meetings. Hughie's kids' piano recitals. Charlotte's Nutcracker performances. Family dinners where my parents did nothing but praise my brother.

I felt like I had this. I could hold out. It wouldn't kill me. Much.

And then.

And then.

I felt one of her hands wandering up my inner thighs. Playing with my balls. Sliding behind them.

Oh, fuck. She wouldn't.

But she did.

She kept up her vicious, glorious sucking on my cock and eased one fingertip into my ass.

Not gonna lie. I came a little bit.

And that fierce little vixen only went at me harder. Pushed that finger all the way in. Relaxed her throat and took me even deeper.

Annnnd that was about it.

I no longer had the capacity to care about bets or my company or the fact that she might not be speaking to me by this time tomorrow. I didn't care that she was getting me back for what I'd done to her ten years earlier in a room at my parents' summer house or that she probably wasn't enjoying this quite as much as she pretended to.

It had been nowhere near five minutes, and it had also been fifteen years.

My vision—gone. My control—gone. My manners—gone.

I took her head in my hands and emptied myself into her throat without a single regret.

She took it. She wanted it. She'd asked for it. And when it was over, she sat back, smiling and gasping for air, dragging a wrist across her mouth.

"That was fun," she said.

Not *I win.* Not *you lose.* Not *I just sucked off a majority ownership in your company* (which she had). But *that was fun.*

My heart—gone.

We had dinner at the inn's restaurant, seated on the outdoor patio. Chloe wore a white sundress that showed off her tanned skin and long dark hair, and I could hardly take my eyes off her.

After dinner we decided to head over to the dunes to watch the sunset. Holding hands, we ambled out along the wooden boardwalk and stood for a few minutes with all the other tourists capturing the moment with selfies, then posting them on social media. But neither one of us even looked at our phone. Tonight was ours alone, and I didn't want to share it with anyone.

We strolled back toward the dunes and took our shoes off to climb up. At the top of the bluff, we dropped down on the sand and watched the sun sink into the lake.

"So beautiful," she murmured with a sigh.

I elbowed her gently. "Glad you came?"

"Yeah. It's been a long time since I did something like this—just sat and watched the sunset. It feels like there's always something to be done at work or at home. No time to sit still."

"I know what you mean. Whenever I sit still, I feel guilty, like there's something I probably should be doing."

"Exactly." She shook her head. "I can't even remember the last vacation I took. Or even the last date I went on."

"Good. Must not have been too memorable."

Laughing, she poked my shoulder. "Jealous?"

"Always." I reached for her, hauling her onto my lap, facing me. "From day one, I hated it when you'd talk about guys."

"I know. I remember. But you talked all the time about girls."

"Well, I didn't want you to think I *liked* you or anything."

"God forbid." The wind blew her hair around her shoulders, and she gathered it in both hands on one side. "We'd spent all those years building up animosity, we couldn't throw all that away just because we were attracted to each other."

"Hell no. What fun would that have been?"

She grinned. "You know, I used to wonder what would have happened on prom night if I hadn't walked away."

"Um, I'd have popped your cherry about four months sooner."

"*Maybe* …"

"Definitely. I wanted you so bad that night."

She laughed. "I'm glad we didn't do it then. I think it would have changed everything."

"Probably," I agreed, thinking back to the way events had unfolded over the years. We definitely didn't have a conventional beginning. "Our story is sort of zig-zagged, isn't it?"

"Yeah, but it's ours," she said, giving up on holding her hair in place and wrapping her arms around me. "And it brought us here, so I like it."

I pressed my lips to hers. "Me too."

Nineteen

Chloe

Now

BACK IN OUR ROOM, I SLIPPED OFF MY SANDALS. "TODAY was magical."

Oliver locked our door and set his wallet and phone on the dresser. "It was."

"I'd forgotten how beautiful it is here. I need to come back more often." I went over to the window and looked out toward the lake, but it was too dark to see anything.

"We'll come back later this summer." Oliver came up behind me and wrapped me in his arms. "How does that sound?"

"Good. Maybe we can go to South Manitou again. Maybe even when they're planting the rye!"

Oliver laughed. "Whenever you want. I'm glad you're excited."

"I am. I really am." Spinning around to face him, I rose up on tiptoe and looped my arms around his neck. "I haven't been this happy and excited about something in forever. Thank you. For asking me to do this with you. For insisting

I listen to you, when all I really wanted to do was punish you."

He tipped his forehead to mine. "I deserved it."

"You did. But I'm ready to forgive you and move on." I smiled. "Maybe the timing wasn't right before. Maybe we still had growing up to do. Maybe if we'd have gone ahead with the plans we made then, we wouldn't be here today. And I think today is pretty fucking awesome." I pressed my lips to his, then jumped up on him, wrapping my legs around his waist.

"It is," he agreed, walking over toward the bed. "And it's about to get even better."

We went slow. Deliciously, torturously slow.

With every article of clothing removed, we lavished time and attention on the skin revealed. The inside of his wrists. The small of my back. The lines on his abs. The curve of my hip. Calf muscles. Collarbones. Chests.

He ran his hands over every inch of my skin as if he'd never touched anything as soft or sexy. He whispered sweet, dirty things in my ear that made me blush. He buried his head between my thighs and used his lips and tongue and fingers on me until I arched and gasped, writhing beneath him with my hands fisted in his hair.

"So was that less than five minutes?" I asked, still panting as he crawled up my body.

"I have no idea. I'm not in a rush this time," he said, bracing himself with his hands above my shoulders.

"Me either." I reached down and took his hot, hard cock in my hands. "But don't make me wait."

I didn't have to worry—he was just as anxious to be inside me as I was to have him there. As his hips rolled over mine, my hands snaked around his back and down over his ass, pulling him closer, deeper, tighter to me.

He went slow until he couldn't hold back anymore, until I was begging him to fuck me harder, until our bodies were so overwhelmed by need they took over, bucking wildly against one another until the tension spiraled so tight and high it snapped, sending us spinning over the edge, soaring head over heels, exploding like stars.

Afterward, we snuggled up with our arms around each other and my head on his chest. I was already falling asleep when I heard his voice.

"Chloe."

"What?"

"I need to say something."

"Okay." I picked up my head and looked at him.

"I've never felt this way about anyone before. And I've never been more sure that something is right. I know it was a risk for you to trust me, but I won't let you down." His crooked grin appeared. "From now on, it's you and me."

Pure joy radiated through me. "Are you trying to make me fall for you, Oliver Pemberton?"

He grinned. "We don't fall. We jump."

I fell asleep with a smile on my face, positive that the risk had been worth it, that my heart had finally led me in the right direction, that people really could change.

This was real. I felt it way down deep.

We spent most of the morning in bed, looking at each other in the sunlight streaming through the window, running our hands along each other's bare limbs, discovering freckles and dimples and scars in hidden places.

"What's this?" I asked, tracing a scar on his ribcage.

"I gouged it on some big rocks in the lake one summer."

"Ouch."

"Yeah, it hurt. But I'd jumped in to save this one kid who'd fallen off the boat, couldn't swim, and wasn't wearing a life jacket."

I gasped. "Oh my God! Are you serious?"

"No." His crooked grin appeared. "But that's a better story than 'I was being a jackass jumping off a rock pile and slipped.'"

I slapped his chest. "Jerk. I believed you."

"I know. You're so gullible."

"Do you even teach sailing to kids or was that bullshit too?" For a moment, I had a small panic attack that I was gullible, and Oliver was still a con man, a wolf in preppy sheep's clothing.

"Yes. I wouldn't lie about that, Chloe. You can take that suspicious look off your face."

"Well, how was I supposed to know? You have to admit, you have a history of stretching the truth when it suits you."

"When did you get this?" he asked me, brushing his thumbs over the long, faintly purple line on my leg, which was hooked over his hips.

"Well," I said, propping my head on my hand, "when I was younger, I used to hang out with this kid who was always daring me to do dumb shit like jump off roofs."

Oliver kissed the scar. "What an asshole. Give me his name, I'll kick his ass."

I smiled at him, narrowing my eyes. "Come on, I don't name names. You know me better than that."

Grinning, he flipped around so that we lay the same way, head to hip to toe. "I do."

I traced the mark on his collarbone. "Funny how we both have a scar from that day. Think it was fate?"

He laughed a little. "Probably. Or stupidity. One of the two."

"I wanted to impress you so badly," I confessed.

"It worked. I was so sure you wouldn't jump."

"So sure that you bet something you didn't even own," I reminded him with a poke on the chest.

He laughed again, and my heart trilled faster at the sound of it. "Sorry. I'll make it up to you someday. Does the leg you broke ever bother you?"

"Not really. I thought about getting a tattoo to cover the scar, but decided against it."

"How come?"

"Well, for one, the scar is kinda badass, don't you think?" I lifted my leg in the air and we both looked at it.

"Definitely," he teased. "If you were coming at me and I saw that scar, I'd think you were scary as fuck."

Slapping him on the chest, I lowered my leg and he caught it, tucking it between his. "And for another," I went on, "it felt like a good reminder that I should look before I leap and all that. It's a lesson I needed to learn. I've always been too hot-headed and impulsive."

"But I love that about you." He threw an arm over my hip and pulled me flush against him. "Don't change."

"Don't worry," I told him. "I'm still that girl on the roof. You dare me to jump, I jump—but you better come with me."

He smiled. "You jump, I jump."

With my heart about to burst from my chest, I looped my arm around his neck and pulled him on top of me. It felt like I'd never be able to get enough of this new Oliver, who had all the best of the old Oliver but who'd matured and changed in ways I could never have anticipated. My feelings for him were ballooning quickly—it was frightening and exhilarating at the same time.

"Oliver," I said breathlessly, when he was inside me again and I felt the last rope tethering my heart to my chest begin to fray. "Tell me it's different this time. Tell me I have nothing to be afraid of."

He picked up his head and looked me right in the eye. "You have nothing to be afraid of. I promise. Everything is going to be perfect."

I believed him.

Around eleven, we finally dragged ourselves from bed. Oliver held my hand as we walked to breakfast in the warm July sun, and I felt an inner calm I hadn't felt in a long time—maybe forever.

But in contrast, Oliver actually seemed a little nervous about something. He kept checking his watch, clearing his throat, rubbing the back of his neck. Over eggs and pancakes, I caught him staring into space with a concerned expression on his face.

"Everything okay?" I asked.

"What? Oh, yeah. Fine." He gave me his usual cocky grin and took another bite of his omelet.

But it happened again while we were waiting for the check. "Hey." I snapped my fingers in front of his eyes. "What's going on in there? Something is on your mind."

He frowned. "Sorry. I think it's just the family thing. I'd rather hang out with you but we have to head to Harbor Springs pretty soon."

"It's fine, Oliver. We'll hang out there for a couple days, and then we can leave. I really don't mind."

"Yeah."

"We should probably head down to Detroit so you can show me around the distillery, right? I mean, I am the majority owner now." I gave his foot a little kick under the table.

That made him smile. "Right. Hey want to walk around the dunes a little more before we hit the road?"

"Sure. If you don't think your mom will be upset we're coming later."

"We'll make it in time for dinner, and that's good enough."

A walk around the dunes turned into another romp in the sack, and we didn't get out of bed until the management banged on the door at three o'clock.

Laughing, we quickly got dressed and hit the road.

"Need anything from home?" he asked me as we approached Traverse City. "We can easily stop."

"No. I have everything I need, and we're late already."

"Are you sure?" He grabbed my hand and kissed it. "I don't mind stopping. Hell, maybe we should skip the cottage altogether and just spend the night alone."

"We can't do that," I chided. "Your parents are expecting us, Oliver. Let's just get there."

He sighed. "Fine."

For a little while, we listened to music and talked about the rye and what steps we'd have to take in terms of the business on paper. Oliver seemed in good spirits, relaxed and happy. But gradually, he went silent, and I noticed the nervous rubbing of his neck again. The furrowed brow. The tight grip of his hand on the wheel.

I wanted to ask him about it, but I didn't want to be

annoying. Family dynamics were complicated, and spending time with everyone under one roof could be stressful. Maybe that's all it was.

Around five o'clock, we drove up the long, winding driveway at his parents' place. There were several other cars parked in front of the house, and Oliver pulled up next to the last car in the row and turned off the engine.

I unbuckled my seatbelt, but before I could open the door, Oliver put a hand on my leg and cleared his throat. "Chloe, there's something I need to tell you."

"What?"

He turned to me and took my hand. "First, I want to say that the past two days have been amazing. I've never been so excited about my life."

"Me neither."

"Like I said, this thing with you and me was not part of my plan when I drove up here, but it was the best surprise ever. I feel like I've been given a second chance I don't deserve, but I'm taking it all the same."

I smiled. "You better."

"And I've meant every single word I've said. I need you to know that."

My stomach flipped over. Not in a good way. "Okayyy."

"Before we go in there—"

"Is that my parents?" Another car had pulled up next to us on the driver's side, and I could have sworn it was my father at the wheel and my mother in the front seat. It looked like their Cadillac too.

"Oh, shit." Oliver looked out the window. "I think it is."

"What are they doing here?"

"My parents must have convinced them to come up for dinner."

Sure enough, my mother hopped out of the passenger seat and waved happily. "Hello there!"

"Hi, Mom!" I called, waving back. Then I squeezed Oliver's hand. "Sorry. Maybe we can finish this talk later?"

"Uh. Yeah." His faced looked a little pale.

"Are you feeling okay?"

"I'm fine." He gave me a smile that was slightly less reassuring than I wanted it to be.

But I opened the door and got out, heading around the car to greet my parents. "What are you guys doing here?" I asked, giving them both hugs.

"Nell called this morning and said we *had* to come up for the night," my mother said as my father pulled their bags from the trunk.

"Oh, really?" I laughed. "I wonder why."

"She said there would be something happening I wouldn't want to miss."

"She did?" I glanced over my shoulder at Oliver, who was grabbing our bags from the back of his SUV. "I wonder what it is."

"Probably just a ruse to get us up here," said my father as he shut the trunk.

"Is April watching the desk?" I asked.

"Yes. Mack and Frannie are both working overtime too," my mother said as we made our way toward the front porch. "I think they even drafted Mack's girls to work."

I laughed as we climbed the steps. "Good. We're going to need extra help. Oliver and I have big plans for Cloverleigh."

"Do you?" My mother glanced back and forth between us, obviously thrilled. "I can't wait to hear about them."

The front door of the cottage flew open and Oliver's

mom appeared. She was slender and maintained her physique with plenty of tennis and golf. Her shoulder-length hair was the same shade of auburn it had been as long as I'd known her, and she always wore it down with a headband that matched her outfit—today it was white shorts, a hot pink cardigan sweater set, Jack Rogers sandals, and pearls. Always pearls.

"Hello, darlings!" she called. "I'm so happy you're all here!"

"Sorry we're late," I said as she embraced me. Her perfume smelled like lilies of the valley. "We got a slow start this morning."

She released me and winked. "I totally understand. Don't worry about a thing, I'm just delighted you're here. I'm delighted about absolutely everything!"

I wasn't exactly sure what she meant, but I smiled. "Me too."

There was a whirlwind of hugs and kisses and greetings. Uncle Soapy came in to give stiff hugs and hearty back slaps. Oliver took our bags upstairs, then came down and took my parents' luggage up as well. Hughie came in to shake my father's hand and kiss my mother's cheek. Aunt Nell shuffled us all through the house and out to the back patio. Through it all, I barely had time to exchange a glance with Oliver, but every time I looked at him, he seemed a little more miserable.

Out on the back patio, Soapy made drinks at the "bar," which was really just a table set up with glasses, ice, and bottles of gin, vodka, scotch, and mixers. The rest of the extended Pemberton family gathered on the patio—Lisa, pregnant Charlotte and her husband Guy, Lisa and Hughie's children, Joel and Toddy, and of course, Gran.

She ambled over, tiny and frail but still stylish in her trousers and blouse, a sweater draped over her shoulders and a strand of pearls around her neck. Her hairstyle was identical to Oliver's mother's, but the color was entirely silver. She held a G & T in one hand and the handle of a cane in the other.

"Hello, Gran. Happy birthday." Oliver dutifully kissed her cheek. "How are you feeling?"

"Never better, darling. Thank you." She turned to me. "So good to see you, Chloe. I couldn't be happier about everything."

Again I wondered what the heck everyone was so happy about—did they know about the business already? "I'm so glad to hear it. Happy birthday." I kissed her cheek. "It's been a while since I've seen you. You're looking well."

She laughed graciously. "Thank you, dear. I try. I've got two new hips now, did Oliver tell you?"

"He didn't." I winked at her. "But you know men. They forget all the important things."

She winked back. "They certainly do. If you just accept that, you can avoid a lot of fights in married life."

"Gran, can I get you a chair?" Oliver asked. "Why don't you come sit down?"

"Thank you, dear, but I think I'm going to go up to my room for a little rest before dinner. I don't want to fall asleep before the excitement."

"Sounds good, I'll help you up the stairs," said Oliver quickly, taking her arm. "Be right back, Chloe."

"No rush." I smiled and let my mother tug me over to the bar, where Uncle Soapy poured me a drink. I sipped it and smiled and chatted with everyone, keeping one eye on the patio door, watching for Oliver.

When he came out about fifteen minutes later, he grabbed a drink from the bar and came over to where I sat with my parents. He took a great big gulp before sitting in the chair next to me.

"Everything okay?" I asked him.

"Everything is great," he said.

But he wouldn't meet my eye.

Everyone wanted to know about our business venture, so we described our trip to South Manitou, regaled them with the story of Jacob Feldmann, told them all about the farm we wanted to purchase, about the heritage rye we wanted to plant, about our plans to build new facilities at Coverleigh in a partnership with Brown Eyed Girl. I blushed listening to Oliver heap praise on my marketing skills, on all I'd accomplished at Cloverleigh, at how thrilled he was I'd agreed to work together.

He went into his usual showman mode as he told the tale of Jacob and Rebecca, and he seemed to recover some of his usual charisma and spark in front of the crowd. We stayed mum about our personal relationship, although he did take my hand at one point, and I know my mother noticed. She and Aunt Nell exchanged what can only be described as an Aren't They Adorable look, as if we were five years old again.

But his leg was twitching beneath the table, and I couldn't shake the feeling that something with him was off.

Twenty

Oliver

NOW

I WAS STARTING TO PANIC.

Somehow, I had to get Chloe alone and tell her the whole story and why it was necessary, but I didn't see how it would be possible before dinner. My mother, who, as predicted, had no poker face whatsoever, was already ushering us from the patio into the house.

"Dinner is nearly ready, everyone," she said. "After you change and freshen up, we'll all meet in the library for cake and champagne in ten minutes. We have to do it before dinner, since Mother gets tired easily. I guess when you're ninety, you get to have dessert before your vegetables!"

Everyone laughed, while I thought, *fuck—ten minutes is not going to be enough time to explain things.*

But it was all I had.

I grabbed her by the hand and tugged her toward the stairs ahead of everyone else. But just as we reached the landing, my mother caught up with us.

"Darlings, I have you together in Oliver's old room,"

she said with a knowing smile. "I hope that's okay. With John and Daphne here too, there weren't quite enough bedrooms for you each to have your own."

"It's fine," Chloe said.

"Normally, I wouldn't put two unmarried people together in a room with Gran here. It's a bit too contemporary for her," my mother whispered. "But I'm a modern woman myself, and I'm sure you two will want to stay together tonight." Suddenly she threw her arms around Chloe. "I'm just so happy. I hope you don't mind I invited your parents. I just thought they should be here for this occasion."

Jesus Christ, Mom.

Chloe looked at me from over my mother's shoulder, her eyebrows rising. No doubt she was confused about what *occasion* this could be. "I don't mind," she said. "It's fun to have everyone together again. It's been a long time."

"It has." My mother released Chloe and looked back and forth between us, her eyes growing misty. "But just think of all the years we'll have to bring the families together."

"We need to go change now, Mom." I grabbed Chloe's hand and began pulling her up the stairs. "We'll see you in the library in ten minutes."

"Don't be late, darling," she called up.

I practically dragged Chloe down the hall to my old bedroom at the cottage, shutting the door behind us. It looked much the same as it had when I was a kid, except the two twin beds were replaced with a queen when I was in high school. Same navy blue and kelly green color scheme. Same sailboat-themed curtains and wallpaper. Same art on the walls—mostly paintings of harbors at sunset.

"Your mom is acting a little strange," Chloe said, going over to her bag, which was on a bench at the foot of the bed. "Don't you think?"

"Uh, yeah." I started pacing back and forth between the bench and the dresser. "But I can probably explain that."

"*You're* acting a little strange too." Chloe looked at me funny as she took off her shoes and unzipped her bag. "Is something wrong?"

My gut was churning, and I ran a hand through my hair. I'd prepared a speech for this, but I couldn't remember a single word of it. Dammit, why'd I drink that scotch on the patio?

"Hey." Chloe came over to me and slipped her arms around my waist. "Talk to me."

I looked down at her concerned expression, at the place where I knew her dimples would appear if she were smiling. And I couldn't bear to think I'd never see them again. This plan had seemed so brilliant before I'd fallen for her.

"It's nothing," I said, hating myself. "I'm just tired after the long drive, and my family can be a bit much."

"Can't everyone's?" She gave me a quick kiss on the chin and went back to rummaging through her bag. "What are you wearing to dinner? Should I wear my dress?"

"Casual is fine."

"I should probably wear the dress," she said with a sigh. "Your mom and grandmother's idea of casual isn't really the same as mine. Do you mind seeing me in it again?"

"Not at all." I watched as she removed her shorts and shirt and bra, slipping the white dress over her head. My blood warmed a little at the sight of her breasts, but I couldn't bring myself to go over and touch her. I didn't deserve it.

"I hope this isn't too wrinkled. Shouldn't you change?"

she asked me, tying the drawstring at her waist. "We only have a few more minutes."

Fuck!

"I have to tell you something," I blurted.

"Okay." She pulled her sandals from her bag, dropped them to the floor, and dug around in her bag some more. "Where's my hairbrush? Did I stick it in here? I hope I didn't leave it at the hotel."

"It has to do with my inheritance," I went on, feeling a sweat break out on my back. I could've sworn I heard the tick of a clock somewhere in the room.

"Oh, there it is." She pulled a brush from her bag and came over to use the mirror above the dresser, standing next to me. "What about your inheritance?"

I swallowed hard. My throat was dry as the fucking desert. "Uh, as you know, I was granted partial access to my trust fund after I finished graduate school, when I was twenty-five. Right before I ran into you in Chicago."

"Right. I remember." She pulled the brush through her long, dark hair in rhythmic strokes.

"And the thing is … I sort of … um, blew it."

She paused with the brush in the air. In the mirror, she met my eyes and blinked. "You blew it? All of it?"

"Pretty much."

"On what?"

The knots in my stomach tightened. "Uh, partying. Playing. Being irresponsible."

"Jesus Christ, Oliver. That had to be a lot of money."

"It was."

"What *possessed* you?"

"I was running away. From family, from responsibility." I swallowed again. "From you."

She didn't say anything.

"I knew I was making a huge mistake, but I didn't want to face it. I just thought, fuck it, if I'm going to mess up my life, I might as well have a good time doing it. I was looking to numb the guilt I felt. It was idiotic and immature, and I'll always regret it."

"So how did you start Brown Eyed Girl?" she asked, turning around and leaning back against the dresser.

"When I finally came to my senses, I returned home and scraped up just enough to get going. The distillery does well, and I think with the expansion it will do even better, but it's going to take some serious cash to implement the plans we've been discussing."

"The land." Chloe came off the dresser, her eyes going wide as she started to panic. "Oh my God, Oliver—if you don't have the money, how are we going to buy the land on South Manitou? How are we supposed to build a facility at Cloverleigh?"

"Don't worry. I have a plan."

It might have sounded more convincing if my voice hadn't cracked on the word *plan*.

"A plan? Oliver, everything hinges on your capital. I don't have anything to invest, and Cloverleigh doesn't have any liquid assets."

I tried to stand taller and speak more confidently. "It's going to be okay, Chloe."

"But we promised the Feldmanns cash up front! Those were our exact words to them. If we have to go through a bank and get a loan, they'll take that other guy's offer, and there goes our land. There goes our story. There goes our hope." She bit her lip. "I wish you would have told me this before."

I took her by the shoulders, forcing her to face me. "Do you still want to do this with me?"

She looked torn. "Well—yes. I mean, I'm not happy you didn't tell me about the money, but …"

Relief rushed through me. Maybe there was still hope. Maybe she'd even think I was a genius for thinking up this idea. "But if I can come up with a way to get it, you're still in?"

She thought for a second, and then she nodded. "Yes, I'm still in. You were an idiot, and you should have told me, but we all make mistakes."

"Thank God." I hugged her tightly. "Leave everything to me. It's going to be fine."

"But how?" she asked. "I still don't understand what we're going to—"

A knock on the door interrupted her, and we moved apart.

"Yes?" I called.

The door opened and my mother appeared in a flowered dress with a sweater around her shoulders and a drink in her hand. "Sorry to bother you. But Oliver, I wondered if you might escort Gran down the stairs into the library?"

Dammit!

"Oh. Sure." Gut churning, I went over to my bag and began rifling through it, trying to think straight, but couldn't. I hadn't gotten to the most critical part of the story yet, and it looked like I might not be able to. "I just need to change."

"All right. She's ready when you are. And she is just beside herself," my mother bubbled. "You've made her the happiest woman alive. She told me you're giving her the only birthday gift she wants."

"You are?" Chloe was giving me a strange look as she pulled on her shoes. "What is it?"

"It's nothing," I said quickly, grabbing a shirt from my bag without even looking at it. "Mom, can you go tell her I'll just be a minute?"

"Sure."

"Is the party in here?" The door opened wider and Chloe's mother appeared.

Jesus fucking Christ, I was *never* going to get Chloe alone.

"Oliver needs to change, so why don't we all go down to the library now?" Chloe looked over at me. "Take your time. I'll see you down there."

"Okay," I said.

What else could I do?

Chloe left the room with our mothers, and I quickly changed my shirt, exchanged my shorts for pants and my sneakers for nicer shoes. I could have used a shave, I thought, checking my reflection in the mirror, but there was no extra time for that. Maybe once I got downstairs, I could pull Chloe aside.

It was my last hope.

Shutting my bedroom door behind me, I hurried down the hall to the guest room where my grandmother always stayed. On the way, I nearly tripped over my nephews, who were playing on the floor with trucks that used to belong to Hughie and me. I ruffled each of their heads before knocking on Gran's door, thinking, *Hughie never would have gotten himself into a mess like this. Neither would Charlotte.*

Gran opened the door and beamed at me. "Hello, dear. Come right in."

I glanced over my shoulder toward the stairs. Hughie and Lisa had come out of their room and were gathering up Joel and Toddy and shooing them down for dinner. I was running out of time. "Don't you want to head downstairs?" I asked Gran.

"In a minute," she said, ambling over to the dresser, where she opened a jewelry box. Then she winked at me over one shoulder. "I need to give you something first, don't I?"

I swallowed hard. "Right now?"

"Well, of course right now. How are you going to propose without the ring?"

My vision blurred, and I leaned on the door frame for support. "I don't know."

"I have it right here. I've been saving it for you." She pulled a ring from the box and held it up. "I don't have the box, of course, but you know, neither did your grandfather when he gave it to me seventy years ago."

I forced myself to walk toward her and take the ring from her fingers.

"He pulled it right from the inside of his jacket pocket and put it on my finger." She looked a little dismayed. "You don't have a jacket for dinner?"

"I'm afraid not."

"Well, I guess you'll do without one." Her smile brightened. "Chloe is so lovely."

"She is." *I hope she doesn't hate me for this.* Carefully I tucked the ring into my pants pocket.

"And I know your grandfather would be so pleased that I saved this ring for you. You were so special to him."

"He was special to me too." Somehow thinking of my grandfather made me feel even worse. What would he think of what I was doing, conning my way into my trust fund so I could buy that land? Or promising Gran I'd propose this weekend as a birthday present? Or pretending as if Chloe and I had secretly been together for a while now? Did it matter that the relationship actually turned out to be real? Would I get a pass on that?

"He always felt you were destined for great things," Gran went on. "And it's okay that it took you a little longer to ground yourself than it took your parents. Or siblings. Or cousins."

"Thanks." I took her arm and guided her from the room. "I'd like to do great things."

"You are! What greater thing is there than starting your own family? And it all begins with choosing a wife."

I cleared my throat as we started down the stairs. "Right."

"You know, that ring had been in the Pemberton family for decades, and when he asked his mother if he could have it for me, his mother said yes. I was considered a pretty good catch, you know."

"I know."

"Just like your Chloe," she whispered. "You hold on to her. And be good. She's not going to take any guff."

"No, she isn't." We were nearly at the bottom of the stairs, and I could hear voices coming from the library. "But listen, Gran. I'm not sure *tonight* is exactly the right night to, you know, pop the question."

"Why is that?"

"So many people around?"

"All the better for a celebration!"

"Uh, we haven't been together very long—just a few months. And we've had to keep it secret, so …"

"Nonsense," she said, tightening her hold on my arm. "You two have always been just right for each other, and you're not getting any younger. It's high time you settled down, Oliver Pemberton, and if you drag your feet, she'll find someone less wishy-washy and settle for him instead. Is that what you want?"

"No, but—"

"Then you get that ring on her finger tonight. Mark my words, she'll be gone if you don't."

We reached the bottom of the stairs and turned for the library. "What if she's not ready?"

"Jiminy cricket, she's thirty-two, Oliver. Of course she's ready."

"Maybe she doesn't want a husband," I tried.

"*Every* girl wants a husband."

I knew that wasn't the case, but Gran was ninety. How could I argue with her?

"And once you're engaged and the wedding date is set," she whispered, "we'll get the remainder of your trust all set up for you so the two of you can buy a house and settle down anywhere you'd like, although your parents and I hope you'll stay close by. You know how I love to dote on my great-grandchildren."

"I know."

"So tonight, then?" she pressed.

I nodded, swallowing hard. "Tonight."

"Good boy." She patted my arm as we entered the library. "Oh, and be a dear and do it before dinner, would you? I get tired and don't always make it to the last course."

"Before dinner?" I almost choked. "Like right *now*?"

"That's a marvelous idea! The library is a beautiful setting." She laughed merrily and pointed to Chloe, who was chatting with Charlotte over by the window. "There she is. Go get her."

My stomach churned even harder as I hurried toward her. "Excuse me. Chloe, can I talk to you alone for a minute?"

"What's with you?" Charlotte asked. "You look like you've seen a ghost. Someone put a rubber snake in your bed?"

Chloe laughed and tipped up her glass of champagne. "God, he was such a little shit, wasn't he? I still haven't forgiven him for that."

"Nor should you ever," Charlotte said.

"We'll just be a minute." I grabbed Chloe's arm and tried to drag her out of the room, but my dad blocked our path.

"And just where do you think you're going?" he boomed. "Grab a glass of bubbly. I'm about to make a toast to your grandmother for her birthday."

"We'll be right back," I said, trying to get around him.

"Oliver, stop it," Chloe hissed, shaking me off. "We can't miss this."

"Chloe, I have to talk to you."

"Later," she told me. "Now go get a glass so we can toast to Gran. She's watching us."

Reluctantly, I went over to the table where a tray of full champagne glasses rested and took one. Then I trudged back over to Chloe and stood next to her, surveying the group assembled. My parents, her parents, Hughie's family, Charlotte and Guy, Gran—they'd all witness my utter humiliation if she said no.

"Are we all here?" my dad asked loudly, looking around. "Everybody have a glass? Good. We've got a lot to celebrate today."

"Hear, hear!" Hughie shouted, which annoyed me for no reason. Did he always have to get a word in?

"Not only are we celebrating our great nation's independence, but we're here to honor my dear mother, who is slightly younger than the United States of America, but no less formidable."

Everyone laughed at the joke, and Gran smiled. "More formidable, some might argue."

"I can attest to that," said my mother, prompting more laughter.

"We also have an upcoming addition to the family," he said, nodding at my sister, "and a new sailboat to christen," he went on, gesturing toward Hughie and Lisa.

"What will you call this one?" Charlotte asked.

"The Lisa Yvonne II, of course," Hughie said, smiling at his wife.

How boring, I thought. As if on cue, Chloe leaned over to me and whispered, "If you ever name a boat the Chloe Lorraine, it's over between us. Ew."

I gave her half a grin. "I was just thinking the same thing. We'll come up with something better." Seeing her suppress a giggle made me feel better. We thought alike in so many ways—she *got* me. She'd get why we had to fake this engagement, wouldn't she?

"I'd also like to toast our lifelong friends, John and Daphne Sawyer," my father orated, lifting his glass in Chloe's parents' direction. "John, here's to your retirement, to your continued success and good health, and to finally getting you to take a holiday off and play some goddamn golf with me. Tee time is nine A.M."

"You're on!" John shouted, raising his glass.

"And finally," my father said, "I'd like us all to raise a glass to a new partnership, both professional and personal. Oliver, your mom and I couldn't be happier for you and Chloe. We've always loved her like a daughter and we can't wait for you to make it official."

Next to me, Chloe made a sort of squeaking noise, and a murmur moved through the room. I caught my grandmother's eye and she nodded, giving me a shrewd smile.

Oh, fuck.

The room spun. My heart raced. My palms felt sweaty. I felt every single eye on me as I turned to face Chloe and set my champagne glass aside. Time was up. If I was going to do this, I had to do it now.

I couldn't fail.

Looking her right in the eye, I dropped to one knee.

Chloe

NOW

No.

This couldn't be happening.

It was too ridiculous. Too farcical. Too absurd. There was no possible way Oliver was going to propose to me right now.

And yet there he was, going down on one knee.

Someone in the room gasped. I nearly dropped my champagne. Oliver looked up at me with a strange mixture of desperation, guilt, and anxiety on his face—*not* the expression you want the guy to have as he asks you to spend the rest of your life with him.

"Chloe," he said, his voice unnaturally loud, like he was on stage. "I know this probably seems sudden."

Sudden? Was he kidding me? We'd only been together for two days!

"But we've known each other all our lives, and no matter how far apart we were, our paths always seemed to lead us back to one another."

Okay, that was true, and kind of sweet, but it still didn't explain what he was doing down on one knee. I'd have asked him, but I was too stunned to talk.

He reached into his pocket and then took my left hand. "You've always been the only one for me, and I hope you'll do me the honor of becoming my wife. Chloe Sawyer, will you marry me?"

"Oh my God," I heard my mother say.

My knees were knocking. My pulse was hammering. My breath was coming too fast. I felt like an actress who'd forgotten all her lines and we'd come to the most climactic scene in the play.

"Uh," I said.

"What?" someone in the room whispered. "Was that yes? Did she say yes?"

I looked around the room in a panic, desperate for an escape hatch.

Oliver squeezed my hand, and I met his eyes again. They were deep and blue and familiar. There was an urgency in them I read immediately as *please go along with this. I need you.*

The fact that we could communicate effortlessly without words tugged at my heart. I was going to fucking kill him for this, but I wouldn't do it in front of his family.

I plastered on a smile. "Yes."

Oliver looked shocked. "Yes?"

"Yes!" I leaned down and kissed him, then whispered in his ear. "Put the ring on my finger, asshole."

He fumbled with it, but eventually managed to slide it onto my fingertip and I shoved it the rest of the way. I stared at it for just a second—it was a beautiful vintage style, Art Deco maybe, with an engraved platinum band and a large round-cut diamond that sparkled in the last rays of the sun slanting through the library window behind me. I held it up for all to see. "I said yes!"

The room erupted with cheers and applause, and Uncle Soapy's voice rang out again. "So let's all drink to health, to happiness, to wonderful years past and all the wonderful years to come. Cheers!"

"Cheers!" everyone echoed, lifting their glasses and taking a sip.

Immediately afterward, we were surrounded by family. Every single person present hugged and kissed and congratulated us. Aunt Nell and Charlotte cried. Gran looked smug. My mother and father were dumbfounded, of course, since they'd seen the way I'd treated Oliver just the other night, but they hugged us both and said how thrilled they were.

"So was that all an act?" my mother said, shaking her head in disbelief. "Had you two been seeing each other in secret? Hiding it from us all?"

I laughed nervously. "We'll explain everything in a minute, I promise." I grabbed Oliver's hand. "I just need a moment alone with my fiancé here."

"Good idea, honey." Oliver took the lead, pulling me out of the library, down the hall, and through a swinging door into the butler's panty.

The minute the door swung shut, I dropped his hand. "What the hell, Oliver? Am I losing my mind, or did we just get *engaged*?" I spoke in the angriest whisper I could manage, but what I really wanted to do was scream.

He held up his palms toward me. "I can explain."

"You damn well better."

"It's about my trust fund."

I stuck my hands on my hips and cocked my head. "What?"

"My trust fund. The money I'll get for hitting this important, mature milestone. Once we're—"

"Oh my *God.*" I shoved his chest, then fisted my hands in my hair. "The money for the land. *This* was your plan? Con your grandmother into thinking we were engaged so she'd give you access to the rest of your trust because you blew the first part of it on hookers and blow?"

Oliver looked offended. "I have never hired a hooker, thank you very much."

"You know what I mean!" I poked at his chest. "You're a con man, and now you're making one out of me."

"We don't have to *con* anybody, Chloe. We're really engaged. I asked you, and you said yes." He grabbed my hand and held it up. "See? There's a ring on your finger."

I yanked it back. "You're unbelievable, and I'm so fucking furious with you, I don't even know where to start. This is not right. And I'm not going to marry you. Not even for a million dollars."

"Why not?"

"Because you *lie*, Oliver. This entire time you've been *lying* to me."

"No, I haven't. I just sort of … revealed the truth slowly. And I was going to tell you about the engagement part, but I didn't get a chance. I swear to God, I had no idea Gran was expecting me to do it so fast."

My confusion from earlier was clearing. "That's what your mother was going on about, all the *special occasion* stuff. That's why she invited my parents. You told them you were proposing today?"

"Well, Gran asked me to. You know, as a birthday gift."

I shook my head. "This is totally ludicrous. How could they fall for it? We haven't even spoken in years."

Oliver winced. "Well, they sort of think we've been seeing each other on the sly for a while."

"What?" I threw both hands in the air. "How are we going to get my parents to believe that? They *saw* us together the other night. I could hardly stand to sit next to you."

"I know. We are the very definition of a love/hate relationship. And we didn't want anyone to know until we were sure it was really love."

"Right now, I am feeling no love, Oliver. You lied. No matter how you try to dress it up, the naked truth is right there in front of me." My throat got tight. "You promised me you were going to be open and honest going forward, and you had a million chances to come clean. You had *days*." As I realized the extent of his deception, my heart began to break. Tears welled in my eyes and spilled over.

Oliver groaned and took me by the shoulders. "Chloe, listen to me. I didn't know what was going to happen between us, and it threw me off. All I wanted was to convince you to see what an amazing opportunity that farm would be. And this was the only way to get it in time."

"Why couldn't you just ask your parents for a loan?"

His face reddened. "Because. I don't want them to know I don't have the money on my own. I never told them about blowing all that money in Europe. I don't want anyone to know that."

"So it's about appearances? That's ridiculous, Oliver!"

He stood taller. "I have my pride, okay?"

"No. It's not okay. We could have gone to the bank."

"If we had to wait for the bank to approve a loan, we'd have lost the land. We need the money in a hurry. All I wanted was to get that farm."

I shook my head. "Bullshit. All you wanted was to trick

me. Make me fall for you so I'd say yes to your stupid plan and then you'd leave me, just like before."

"You're wrong," he said forcefully.

I couldn't even talk for a moment. Little pieces of the puzzle were snapping into place, and the big picture wasn't pretty. Had I been a fool for him again? Was I just a pawn in his game? Did he care about me at all, or was I simply the shortest route from him to his big fat inheritance?

"Christ," I said, fighting back sobs. "I'm such an easy mark. You knew the whole time. You knew when you approached my father last month. You knew driving up here. You knew I'd fall for you again and you used it against me. You said it once before—I'm so fucking predictable."

"That's not true! I had no idea you and I would pick up where we left off."

I swiped at my eyes. "You wouldn't know the truth if it came up and bit you. And we didn't *leave off*, Oliver, *you left me*. You tricked me into believing you were someone else in Chicago, someone who actually cared about me, and then you disappeared. You did it then, and you're doing it now."

"I'm not! Chloe, please. Think of all the plans we've made over the last few days. We've had this dream for a long time, and it's within our reach. I'm willing to do whatever it takes to get there. Aren't you?"

We heard noise in the hallway as the family made their way into the dining room. I knew we'd have to make an appearance shortly, but I felt like I might have to vomit first.

"I feel sick, Oliver. What are we supposed to do? Go out there and pretend to be in love?"

"Well … yes." He let his arms fall.

I shook my head. "I don't know if I can do it."

"Can you try? Please?"

"And then what? I'm not going through with this ridiculous charade engagement, Oliver. You don't love me. You don't want to marry me. You just wanted your money."

"It isn't like that, Chloe, I promise. I do love you." He went to take me in his arms but I put my hands out to stop him.

"Your promises mean nothing to me now. And you don't love anyone but yourself. You never have." Taking a step back, I gave myself a few deep breaths, refusing to acknowledge the devastated look on his face. It was probably fake, anyway.

"I'll go out there and get through dinner, but that's it. Tomorrow, I'm leaving with my parents and you're going to come clean to your family."

"But what about the money? What about the land and the rye? What about our dream?"

Sobs threatened again, but I swallowed them back and stood taller. "My self-respect is more important. You'll have to find another way to get your money. I'm out."

I spun around and pushed the swinging door open, praying for the strength to get through the next hour and a half.

Before going to the dinner table, I darted up the stairs to my room to fix my face a little. There was no way to hide the fact that I'd been crying, but I figured a few tears were normal after getting engaged. I did what I could and headed down to the dining room.

"There she is," Gran crooned when I walked in.

Oliver was already seated at the table, which was set for thirteen but could easily have seated twenty. The only empty place was between Oliver and Charlotte, and I did my best to put a smile on my face as I moved toward it. "Sorry to keep you waiting."

"That's okay." Oliver jumped up and pulled out my chair.

Ever the gentleman. All part of his act.

But I sat down and let him push me closer to the table, holding my breath as he took his place beside me. I didn't want to catch his scent for fear I'd burst into tears. As it was, I had to avoid looking at my left hand, where that beautiful ring circled my finger, reminding me what an idiot I'd been.

Right away, my parents wanted to know how we'd pulled off our secret relationship. Over a first course of Waldorf salad, I attempted to explain, grateful for the summer theater camps I'd done as a kid when my parents needed a safe place for me to release energy.

"It was tricky," I said. "We didn't see each other very often, and I had no idea he was talking to Dad about my distillery plans."

"I like to keep her on her toes," Oliver said.

"And I like to make sure he doesn't take it for granted that I'll go along with what he says," I shot back.

Uncle Soapy laughed heartily. "Sounding like an old married couple already, aren't they? I'd say you've met your match, Oliver."

"I'd say so too, Dad." Oliver peeked at me, and I tried to take some of the murder out of my gaze.

It wasn't easy.

Over lobster, corn, green beans, and fresh bread, I managed to answer everyone's questions with what I hoped was convincing ease, laugh at Oliver's jokes, say a few nice things about him, and even look at him adoringly a few times. I might not have been the actor he was, but by the time we ate cake and ice cream, I was pretty sure no one suspected the engagement was just a scheme. Even Gran managed to last through the entire meal, smiling benevolently in our direction the whole time.

The food was delicious, but I barely touched it. All I could think of was how we were lying to everyone we loved—*for money*.

When the dessert plates were cleared, Lisa took the boys up to bed, Gran retired to her room, and the other adults moved into the family room to play cards. I followed them, but I didn't want to stay.

"What do you say, Chloe? Feel like some bridge or euchre?" Oliver asked.

"No, thanks. I'm actually not feeling very well. I think I'll go to bed. Thanks for dinner, Aunt Nell. It was delicious."

"You're welcome, dear. Get some rest." She came over and kissed my cheek. "Maybe tomorrow while the boys are golfing, your mom and you and I can sit down and talk wedding planning."

"Oh, yes, let's!" said my mother from her place at the card table. "I can't believe I have two daughters to plan weddings for now."

"Maybe you shouldn't retire this year, John," teased Uncle Soapy. "With two weddings to pay for and all."

My father groaned. "I might have to sell the farm."

"Don't worry, Dad," I assured him. "You'll be all right. Goodnight, everyone."

"I'll go up with you," Oliver said, following me out of the room.

I wanted to argue but held my tongue until we were going up the stairs. "You don't have to babysit me. I won't give away your secret. I'll leave that for you after I'm gone."

"Chloe, please. Can't we talk about this some more?" he whispered as we went down the hall.

"No."

"This whole thing was a shock, I know. But doesn't your therapist want you to think things over before acting too rashly?"

I stopped to face him, giving him a look of pure disbelief. "You cannot be serious. My therapist is trying to keep me from making horrible mistakes, like jumping into bed with you. Like trusting you. Like falling for your act and thinking you've changed."

"I have changed, Chloe."

Shaking my head, I continued moving down the hall. "I will never believe another word you say."

He followed me into the bedroom and silently shut the door behind him. "Can you at least just take the night to think it through?"

"I don't need the night." I pulled off the ring and laid it on the dresser before slipping my shoes off. "And you're not sleeping in this bed with me."

"Where am I supposed to sleep? All the bedrooms are taken."

I shrugged as I walked over to my bag, where I began hunting for my pajamas. "Figure something out. I don't want you in here."

"Chloe." He walked toward me slowly. "Look at me, please."

I didn't want to. I had a tender spot for him and he knew it. "Leave me alone, Oliver."

"Give me another chance."

I forced myself to meet his eyes. They appeared to reflect contrition and remorse, but I no longer trusted my assessment of his feelings. He was too good at the game. "You don't deserve another chance."

He sighed heavily. Nodded once.

In a moment, I was going to break down, but for now I steeled myself. "I'm going to the bathroom to change. When I come back, I want you gone. And take that ring with you—put it somewhere safe so you can give it back to your grandmother after I leave."

He said nothing as I walked into the bathroom and shut the door.

Once I was alone, I gripped the sink and let the tears flow as silently as I could. I didn't want him to hear me crying. I didn't want him to know how badly he'd hurt me. I didn't want him to know how much I'd miss his arms around me for the rest of my life or how devastated I was that all the plans we'd made would never see the light of day.

God, how could I have been so stupid?

Angrily, I grabbed a tissue from the box on the back of the toilet and blew my nose. Hadn't I known before all this started that he could not be trusted? His entire life, when had he ever demonstrated that he cared about anyone other than himself? He'd never once stuck around long enough to develop real feelings for anyone, least of all me. He was a cad and a player and a con man who got through life on his lies and his charm, and he was never going to change. I'd known it all along.

So this was on me, I thought, as I looked at my mascara-streaked face in the mirror with its red nose and bloodshot eyes. Once again, I'd shown what shitty judgment I had. I'd jumped into something without considering the big picture. I'd let myself be swept away by pretty words and dreams because it felt good. It was like teenage me all over again. Had I learned nothing?

I wasn't fit to be CEO of Cloverleigh or my own business. I was a terrible judge of character and had no idea how to control my impulses. No matter how much therapy I had or how much growing up I did or how strongly I felt things in my gut, *I could not be trusted to do the right thing.*

The realization hit me hard and brought on fresh tears that wrenched sobs from my chest. I sat down on the edge of the tub and cried hard for myself, for my crushed dreams, for my broken heart.

I couldn't sleep.

I lay there alone in Oliver's old bed in the dark for hours. Awake. Empty. Aching.

I missed him. I missed the excited feeling I'd woken up with this morning. I mourned the dreams we'd shared.

What if I never got over him? What if I never met anyone else who pushed my buttons the way he did? What if no one else ever *got to me* the way he did? Was I destined to live alone, cursing him and his stupidity for the rest of my life? Was he?

Relationships were fucking hard, and I'd never been able to make it work with someone, never known that feeling of contentment and security. I'd never let myself be as vulnerable as I'd been over the last few days—and I never would again. It hurt too much to know it had been a mistake.

God, Oliver. We came so close.

The old house was creaky in the wind, and more than once I heard strange noises that made my eyes pop wide open and my heart beat faster. I'd never liked being alone in the dark.

When I heard rain begin to drum against the windowpane, I got up and turned the bathroom light on, leaving the door partway open just to give me a little bit of light. On my way back to bed, I caught sight of something shiny on the dresser.

The ring.

I hadn't noticed it before, when I'd fallen into bed exhausted and cried out. Why hadn't he taken it with him when he'd left, like I'd asked?

I walked over to the dresser, the old wood floor creaking under my bare feet. Picking up the ring, I stared at it for a moment before slipping it onto my finger again. Then I examined it on my hand, fingers outstretched.

Oliver, I thought, my broken heart sinking deeper. *You bastard.*

I would have said yes.

That's what killed me. I knew myself. And I knew how I felt about him. If I was honest, I had to admit that if there had been no games, no scheme to get the money, no betrayal of my trust, and Oliver had said to me last night, maybe as he held me in his arms or moved inside me or kissed me goodnight, *I've always loved you, spend the rest of your life with me* … I would have said yes. It would have been crazy and fast and impulsive, but it was the truth.

I climbed back in bed and wept into my pillow.

I would have said yes.

Twenty-Two

Oliver

NOW

I HEARD HER CRYING IN THE BATHROOM, AND IT DAMN NEAR broke me.

The moment she shut the door, I heard the gut-wrenching gasps, and I immediately rushed in her direction.

But I stopped with my hand on the knob.

She doesn't want you. You'll only make things worse.

My hand fell, and I backed away.

What was I going to say to her that I hadn't already said? How was I going to make this better? Which words were the ones to make her see that I hadn't lied to her, that I wanted to be with her, that I'd made a mistake, yes—but I was human and still figuring shit out.

I loved her. I'd never loved anyone the way I loved her. Shouldn't that count for something?

I felt like it should, but I also felt like she was right—I didn't deserve another chance.

Backing away from the door, I glanced at the ring on

the dresser. She'd told me to take it with me when I left.

I walked over to it and picked it up, recalling the cringe-worthy proposal and the clumsy way I'd struggled to get the ring on her finger.

Fuck. What had I been thinking? She deserved so much better.

A better proposal. A better love story. A better man.

I replaced the ring on the dresser and left the room. In the end, I couldn't bring myself to take it. Maybe she wouldn't wear it on her finger, but I wasn't sorry I'd given it to her. And maybe if I left it here, she'd know that I'd meant what I said.

She'd always been the only one for me.

When I went downstairs, I avoided the family room where the card games were going on and instead went into the library. Shutting the door behind me, I turned off the light and lay down on the leather couch in front of the fireplace. I knew I wouldn't be able to sleep, but at least this was a quiet place to think.

With one hand behind my head, I stretched out on my back and let the memories of my friendship with her unspool. I saw us as kids jumping off that roof. I saw us as teenagers at the prom. I saw her sitting on my dorm room bed asking me to have sex with her, telling me she wanted me to take her virginity but not call her afterward—even then, she didn't trust me with her heart.

She'd been right.

I saw her devastated expression the following Christmas, when I'd lied to her, saying that I'd only done it because I'd pitied her. I'd wanted to hurt her because she didn't want me the way I wanted her, and I was too young and stupid to see that I should have been honest with her instead of playing games.

I saw her laughing and rosy-cheeked as we got tipsy on scotch between two twin beds at Hughie's graduation party. I saw her standing above me, a leg over my shoulder, as I buried my tongue inside her. I saw her back as she angrily stomped away from me down the hall after realizing I'd timed her orgasm.

That memory actually brought a smile.

I saw her standing at the bar in a gorgeous gown at a hospital fundraiser, I saw her hesitate before getting onto that elevator with me, I saw her naked and sweaty and shameless against a hotel room door.

I remembered a cab ride to the airport after we said goodbye in Chicago, hating myself for being too immature and unworthy of her.

I saw her give me the finger at a Cloverleigh Christmas party. I felt the sting of her palm across my cheek. I heard the hurt and anger in her voice as she accused me of betraying her with Brown Eyed Girl.

I saw the wary suspicion in her eyes as I persuaded her to give me one week to convince her to partner with me. I heard her say, *Some things don't change. Some people don't change.*

Maybe she was right. Maybe I was the same selfish asshole I'd been all those years. I'd fucked up so many times. How many chances did one man deserve?

And what could I say to get her to give me another?

I wasn't sure how long I lay there in the dark, but eventually I heard everyone else go up to bed, and a while later,

I heard the rain begin. It drummed against the library windowpanes, the wind pressing against the glass. When lightning flashed and thunder began to rumble in the distance, I thought of Chloe alone upstairs and wondered if she was nervous. I knew she didn't like storms or the dark. Imagining her up there alone and scared made my chest tight.

Leave her be. She doesn't want you.

But eventually I couldn't stand it anymore.

I got up from the couch and hurried quietly from the library, up the stairs, and down the hall. When I reached my old bedroom door, I hesitated for just a second, but then opened it.

I saw right away that she'd left the bathroom light on and the door ajar, and it wrenched my heart. Lightning illuminated the room for a moment, and I saw that she was asleep, lying on her side with her left hand on the pillow next to her face.

There was something shiny on her finger.

Had it been a trick of the light, or was she wearing the ring? Hoping she wouldn't wake up and catch me lurking over her in bed like a stalker, I moved closer, my stomach muscles tight.

Sure enough, my grandmother's engagement ring was back on her finger. She must have put it on after I left the room. My heartbeat quickened. Did that mean she didn't hate me? That she still cared? That she might be willing to listen to me?

But what the hell would I say?

If I trusted myself to find the right words, I might have crawled into bed with her. Put my arms around her. Stopped her protests with a kiss.

But I didn't.

In the end, I backed out of the room and shut the door behind me, retreating downstairs again to face my night of purgatory on the couch.

I must have fallen asleep at some point because it was light when my dad woke me, sunlight streaming through the windows. "Something wrong with your bed?" he asked.

Opening my eyes, I saw him standing over me dressed in his golf clothes, glass of orange juice in his hand. I groaned as I sat up, my back stiff and my neck sore. "Uh, I gave it to Chloe. She felt funny staying in the same room."

He nodded, apparently satisfied with the explanation. "We're heading out in about half an hour for golf. Are you joining us?"

"Maybe." I turned my head to the right and left, trying to ease some of the tension. "Is Uncle John still going?"

"Yes. Why wouldn't he?"

"No reason." Actually, the reason was that I wondered if Chloe had convinced her parents to go back home to Cloverleigh first thing this morning. "Let me check with Chloe, see what she wants to do today."

I went upstairs to find my bedroom empty, the bed made, her bag packed.

My heart sank.

But when I looked at the dresser, the ring wasn't there. Somehow, it gave me hope, even though I knew she was probably only wearing it to keep up appearances until she could leave.

I took a quick shower, changed into clothing appropriate for golf, and went down to the kitchen, wondering what she was going to say to me.

The kitchen was empty, but I heard voices coming from the patio. I poured a cup of coffee and followed the sound.

"Good morning, sleepyhead," called my mother. She, Aunt Nell and Chloe were sitting at the table under the umbrella, cups of coffee, and plates of fruit and muffins in front of them. I noticed Chloe hadn't touched her breakfast. She'd hardly eaten a thing at dinner last night either. Guilt sat heavily on my shoulders.

"Morning, everyone." I tested the waters by taking the seat next to her, but she didn't protest.

"Are you golfing with the boys today?" my mother asked.

"I thought I might. If it's okay with you," I said to Chloe.

"It's fine," she said stiffly, barely giving me a glance. She wore sunglasses, so I couldn't see her eyes.

"Okay, then I guess I will." I took a sip of my coffee. "What will you ladies do today?"

"Oh, don't worry about us." My mother waved her hand in a dismissive gesture. "We've got plenty of talking to do about the wedding, and we might wander into town, do some shopping. Later, we might spend some time in the pool. It's going to be a beautiful day."

"Sounds like fun." I attempted to smile, but the icy silence on my right was discouraging. Maybe it meant nothing that she'd put the ring on again last night.

When she excused herself from the table only a few minutes after I sat down, I got up and followed her, leaving my coffee on the table.

She didn't say anything until we reached the kitchen, which was empty. "What do you want, Oliver?"

"To talk to you."

She dumped her uneaten breakfast in the trash and set her plate in the sink. "About what?"

"About everything." But now that we were alone, I didn't know what to say. "How did you sleep?"

"Fine." She turned around and leaned back against the counter, pushing her sunglasses to the top of her head. "You?"

"Shitty."

"Where did you end up?"

"On the couch in the library."

She nodded, crossing her arms over her chest. She wore shorts that showed off her tan, muscular legs, and my entire body ached, thinking that I'd never be close to her warm, bare skin again. "You can have the bed tonight. I'm hoping to convince my parents to leave before dinner."

"Chloe, don't go." I moved toward her and thought she'd duck away, but she didn't. I put my hands on her shoulders. "I'm sorry. I want to work this out. I know what I did was wrong, but the important thing was to get the money."

She shook her head. "Are you even listening to yourself? This is how you blew your money the first time, Oliver. You can't go through life only thinking about short-term gratification. Your decisions have consequences. They hurt people, and this plan to trick everyone you love is cruel."

"This wouldn't have hurt anybody. People break up all the time. It's not like it was a real relationship." I realized what I'd said and frowned. "I mean, it wasn't supposed to be."

A tear slipped down her cheek. "Nothing changes. You're still the same old Oliver."

"No! Look, I'm sorry I wasn't up front with you. I'm sorry I withheld the full truth. I'm sorry I don't do everything right the first time." I paused. "Or the second time.

But I'm not perfect, Chloe—I just wanted to build something of my own. I wanted to grow something, create something. And I wanted to do it with you. I still do."

"It's too late," she said, wiping her eyes. "It's too late." Then she pushed me away, and rushed from the room.

Exhaling, I braced my hands on the edge of the counter and hung my head.

It was hopeless.

I'd lost it all.

I decided against golfing with the rest of the guys. There was no way I'd be able to enjoy it, and I didn't have the energy or the desire to pretend. Despite what Chloe thought of me, I wasn't that good an actor. Instead, I told my father I wanted to take the boat out and drove down to the marina without saying a word to anyone else.

Last night, I'd spent hours going over the past, revisiting all my mistakes. Out on the water today, I thought about my future. What I really wanted. Where I'd end up. How I would get there.

As a kid, I had imagined myself with a life exactly like every other adult man I knew—a life as a husband, a father, a career Pemberton man with a corner office and a closet full of Brooks Brothers suits. But when it came time to choose those things, I hadn't chosen them. Somehow deep down, I'd never wanted to go down that path.

Not that there was anything wrong with it. My parents were happy. My brother and sister were happy. I still saw myself as a father someday. But I'd always been convinced there was something *more*.

The weekend Chloe and I spent in my Chicago hotel room, I'd felt certain I'd found it, and maybe I had. It choked me up a little thinking that I'd been right back then, but too scared to go after it.

Because what if I'd failed? What if I wasn't the man she thought I was? What if I wasn't destined for great things or worthy of a girl like Chloe, or deserving of a life out of the ordinary?

I'd never felt so much self-doubt before, so I'd run from it, and from her. Then I'd been so ashamed of myself, I'd stayed away. I saw my engagement to Alison as a sort of punishment—I'd blown my chance with the girl I really wanted, so I should be forced to endure a lifetime with someone I couldn't stand, right?

Even now, when I looked back at my grand scheme to get the rest of my trust, I could see the ways that shame and self-doubt had fueled my behavior. I was too proud to go to my father, admit my mistakes, and ask for a loan. I was too worried about looking foolish compared to my brother. I was too concerned with what everyone else would think of a guy like me—a guy who'd been handed every single advantage in life and still managed to fuck it up.

Looking ahead, I had no idea what would happen. I supposed I'd have to cover for myself once Chloe left, find some way to explain the breakup to my family, and look for another way to raise the money to buy the land, expand Brown Eyed Girl, and craft a heritage rye.

But it all seemed pointless without her. I hardly cared anymore. It made me wonder if all along what had been driving me to chase this dream was the desire to be with her rather than money or accolades or pride.

Maybe the dream had always been her.

Chloe

NOW

I spent the day with my mother and Aunt Nell, although I can't say I enjoyed it. All they wanted to talk about was Oliver and me, how cute it was that we'd finally fallen in love, how right they'd been all along about what a good match we'd make, what good secret-keepers we were to have hidden our relationship so well. They spoke of wedding dresses and bridal showers and guest lists. Music and food and flowers. Invitations and photography and memories of their own weddings, at which they'd stood up for one another as maids of honor.

It was agony.

All I could think was that I'd never have any of those things.

Worst of all, my mother refused to consider leaving early.

"But we're always so busy this week of July," I'd protested. "Is it really fair to leave April and Frannie with such a big burden?"

"It's fine," she said, patting my shoulder as we window-shopped. "I just spoke to April this morning, and she said all was well."

"You didn't say anything about the engagement, did you?" I asked.

She sighed. "No, but it was very difficult. You're going to tell them when we get home, right? I don't know how long I can keep such a juicy secret."

I nodded, feeling sick to my stomach again. "Sure."

When we got home, my mother and Aunt Nell decided to sit around the pool with Charlotte, Lisa, and the boys, but I said I was feeling tired and wanted to lie down.

"You've been awfully tired over the last twenty-four hours," my mother remarked as she tucked a few things into her pool bag. "You're looking a bit pale too. And you haven't eaten much either." She looked up, her expression a mix of excitement and alarm. "Are you pregnant?"

Rolling my eyes, I leaned against the door frame of her room. "I'm not pregnant, Mom. I'm just tired. It's been a crazy week."

She didn't look entirely convinced, and I could only imagine that she and Aunt Nell would sit around the pool naming their future grandchildren. But she left me alone and went out to the pool, and I went to my room by myself.

The first thing I did was remove the ring and place it on the dresser. My throat closed up, but I left it lying there and curled up on the bed. I'd only been resting there a few minutes when I heard a knock on the door.

Oliver.

I sat up quickly. "Yes?"

The door opened slowly, and Gran stood there. "Hello, dear."

"Oh. Hello." I was surprised at the disappointment I felt. I should have been glad Oliver had given up on me and taken off to go sailing alone, right?

"May I come in?" Gran asked.

"Sure."

Using her cane, she ambled into the room and moved toward the only chair, which was next to the dresser. Right away, I realized she'd see the ring on the otherwise bare dresser top.

Sure enough, she paused a moment to look at it before lowering herself into the floral-upholstered chair. "And where's our Oliver today?"

"I'm not sure." I fidgeted with my empty ring finger. "I think he was going to go sailing."

A strange silence followed. I had no idea what to say.

Gran was studying me with shrewd eyes. "You don't want to marry our Oliver, do you?"

I thought about lying. In fact, I opened my mouth to do it. But I couldn't. Instead I shook my head, feeling shame paint my cheeks.

She nodded as if she'd known. "But you love him."

Again, I thought of giving a false answer, but I didn't. "Yes," I said quietly, looking down at my hands. "I can't help it."

"Even after what he's done?"

I looked up at her in surprise. "What he's done?"

"Oh my dear, you don't survive to be ninety without becoming a pretty good judge of character. And Oliver isn't quite the actor he thinks he is."

"Well, he fooled me," I admitted. "I thought he really cared about me, but all he really wanted was the money."

"I'm not sure that's true," she said. "In fact, I'm fairly

certain he does care for you, even more than he knows." She paused to sigh. "Which is why I didn't think he'd go through with that silly proposal last night. I thought by pressuring him to do it so quickly, he'd buckle and tell me the truth."

"Oliver has a tricky relationship with the truth," I said bitterly. "He only embraces it when it suits him."

"You're right about that."

"And he's gotten away with it his whole life!"

"We can blame his mother for that," Gran said drily. "I love my daughter, but Jiminy Cricket, she spoiled him rotten."

I had to laugh a little. "She did."

"And he's got more charm than any one man should be allowed to have."

"Agreed," I said, shaking my head. "I don't know what it is about him, but he gets to me every time. Even when I know he's not playing by the rules, I—"

"Can't help wanting to play along?" Gran winked at me. "I know just what you mean. I was married to a charmer too. What they need is a good, strong woman to keep them in line."

I nodded. "Exactly."

"You know, everyone thinks I'm old-fashioned and stubborn about tradition, and maybe I am, but I'm a feminist in my own way. And I think you're right to tell Oliver to go to the devil. How dare he assume he could prop you up as his fiancée and fool me in the process?" She clucked her tongue. "What a donkey's ass."

The curse word made me laugh. "I agree."

"The question is," she went on, "what are we going to do with him? Do you think this scheme of his with the Russian rye is malarkey or the real deal?"

"I think it's the real deal," I said honestly. "He's onto something."

"So you think I should give him the money?"

I blinked at her. Was she really asking me if she should give Oliver a million dollars? "I'm not sure I'm qualified to give that answer."

"Sure you are. Be confident. Trust your gut. If it was your money, would you buy that land?"

"Yes. I would. Oliver has done the research. He's got talent and experience, and he knows the market. He's made mistakes in the past," I hedged, not wanting to say too much.

She waved a hand. "Oh, I know all about the way he burned through his money in Europe, the damn fool."

"You do?"

She tapped her head. "Ninety. Remember?"

I laughed. "Right. Well, like I said, he's made mistakes, and this whole fake engagement thing is the worst idea he ever had, but he knows what he's doing. If he could get that land, he'd achieve everything he wants to, I have no doubt."

"With *or* without you?"

I thought for a moment. "I don't know. When he approached me about partnering with him, he made me feel like he needed me, but … I have no idea if he meant what he said."

"Oh, I think he did. I heard the way he went on about you last night. And I saw the way he looked at you. That wasn't acting. But let me ask you this." Gran regarded me thoughtfully. "If he had the money to buy the land, would you still partner with him?"

My eyes filled, and I shook my head. "I don't think so," I said, my throat catching.

"Because you can't trust him?"

"That, and … because I love him," I whispered, unable to speak.

She nodded once. "Well, you've given me a lot to think about. I'll leave you now and take my siesta as well." She rose to her feet with such ease that I almost wondered if the cane was for show.

Gran was one sharp cookie.

At the door, she turned around. "You'll be at dinner tonight?"

"Yes. I wanted to leave today, but my mother refused. She doesn't know …" I trailed off.

"What's the plan for that?" she asked.

"I told Oliver I'd keep up the act while we were here, but that he had to come clean to you all once I'd left."

"Awfully generous of you. More generous than he deserves."

I lifted my shoulders, feeling my throat tighten again.

"I know," she sighed. "He's a donkey's ass, but he's the donkey's ass you love. I'll see you this evening."

She pulled the door shut behind her, and I was alone again.

I lay back, but I was restless and fidgety, my thoughts a jumbled mess and my feelings even more tangled up. Finally, I gave up, dug my phone from my purse, and called April.

"Hey, Chloe," she said when she answered.

"Hey. You busy?"

"Not too bad. We're in sort of that afternoon lull. What's up?"

I groaned and flopped onto my back. "I don't even know where to start."

She laughed. "Beginning?"

"That's too far back—like the day I was born. It's fucking Oliver."

As quickly as I could, I got her up to speed on the last couple days, sparing no details. By the time I finished, I imagined her on the floor at the reception desk, open-mouthed in shock.

"Oh my God," she said when I'd finished telling her about the conversation with Gran. "I can't believe she knew he was faking it. And she still gave him the ring!"

"I know." I sat up and looked at it on the dresser, sort of surprised she hadn't taken it when she left. "I guess I have to keep wearing it too. At least for one more night. It just feels so wrong."

"I'm so sorry, honey."

"You know what the worst thing is?" The ceiling became blurry as tears filled my eyes. "I keep wondering if that stupid fake proposal is the only one I'll ever get."

"It's not, Chloe."

"Like, I've never even cared," I said, wiping my eyes. "I've never been that girl obsessed about getting married. But I was standing there looking down at him on one knee, listening to him say these sweet words in front of an audience, and it really sucks that I don't even know if he meant them."

"I bet he did, deep down. Think of all the things he said to you without an audience. He meant those, don't you think?"

"I have no clue." I squeezed my eyes shut and forced myself to quit crying. "But whatever. I guess I'll never have any clue."

"So there's no way to salvage it?" she asked. "Even though you still have feelings for him?"

"I don't see how." I took a deep, shuddering breath, and faced the truth by saying it out loud. "He wants that money more than he wants me, April. Otherwise, he'd have told the truth already."

She had no reply.

"I'm sorry, sis. This is hard." She sighed. "And we're starting to get busy in here so I better go."

"Okay. I'll see you tomorrow. Thanks for listening."

We hung up, and I curled back into a ball on my side, wondering how I was going to get through the night.

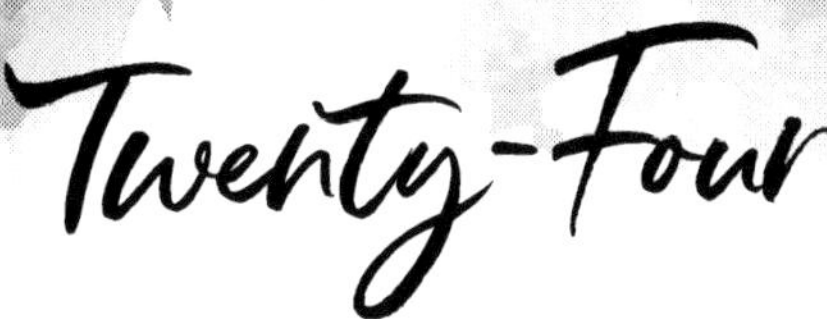

Twenty-Four

Chloe

NOW

"I JUST DON'T UNDERSTAND WHY HE'S SO LATE," AUNT Nell complained. "He knows what time dinner is. Why didn't he come back sooner?"

We were in the library having cocktails and Oliver still hadn't shown up yet. I'd have been worried about him sailing alone except that he'd texted me that he was running late because he had to run an errand.

That was not sitting well with his mother.

"Honestly, that boy has no sense of urgency about anything at all," she went on, sitting down next to me on the couch. "I should have taught him better. He'll probably be late to his own wedding."

I tried to smile, but it was difficult. I'd been sitting there sipping some scotch and staring at the ring on my hand, getting more and more despondent by the minute. Tomorrow it would be returned to Gran, and I'd go home alone.

It was what I wanted. So why did it hurt so much?

I was about to excuse myself from the room because I

was afraid of bursting into tears again, when I heard Oliver's voice behind me

"Sorry I'm late," he said loudly.

I looked at him over my shoulder—he was dressed in the same clothing he'd been wearing all day, appearing sun-tanned and windblown and gorgeous.

"Oliver, what on earth are you wearing?" his mother asked. "Go change for dinner, please. And good grief, run a comb through your hair."

"No." He strode further into the room, all the way to the fireplace, and stood in front of it. All eyes were on him. "Sorry I'm late, Mom, and I know your rule about T-shirts at the dinner table, but what I have to say is more important than how I look saying it."

I blinked at him in surprise.

"In fact, I owe all of you an apology," he said. "I lied to you. And what's worse is that I forced Chloe to lie too." He met my eyes. "I'm sorry, Chloe."

Chills swept across my skin. My jaw dropped.

"I don't understand," said Aunt Nell.

"Let me explain." Oliver took a breath. "I needed money to buy that land I told you about yesterday, and I was too proud to admit I didn't have it on my own and ask for a loan."

"Why would you need a loan?" Hughie asked from behind me somewhere.

Oliver grimaced. "That's kind of another story. Suffice it to say, my bank account isn't as big as it would be if I'd made better decisions in my twenties. So my plan was to ask Chloe to agree to a fake engagement so I could inherit the remainder of my trust fund from Gran."

"Oh my God." Aunt Nell covered her mouth with her hand. "Oliver Ford Pemberton, you didn't."

Oliver nodded, his mouth set in a line. "I did. But Chloe didn't know about it. Before I could explain things to her, the situation got away from me. So she was totally in the dark when I asked her to marry me last night."

Aunt Nell looked at me. "Is this true?"

"Yes," I said, my voice and my knees trembling. The rest of me felt like I was having an out-of-body experience. Was this really happening?

"But you said yes!" Aunt Nell exclaimed. "Why did you say yes?"

"She said yes to cover for me," Oliver answered, and I was glad he did. My throat was so tight.

"So ..." She grabbed my arm. "So you're not really in love?"

My mother, who was seated adjacent to me in a leather club chair, sat up straight and touched her heart.

I looked at Oliver.

"We are," he said emphatically, his eyes locked on mine. "At least, *I* love *her*, and I hope that she can find it in her heart to forgive me and give me another chance. Not that I deserve it."

"No. You don't."

Everyone looked at Gran, who'd uttered the words. She sat over to the right of the fireplace in a tall wingback chair, looking imperious and unhappy—but not shocked.

"I'm sorry, Gran," Oliver went on. "I knew better. My parents taught me better. Grandpa expected better."

His voice wavered, and my heart ached. I knew how he'd loved his grandfather.

"Yes, he did," Gran said. Then her voice softened. "But he wasn't perfect, either."

Oliver shook his head and looked at me again. "Chloe

said yes last night because she could see how humiliated I'd be if she'd said no. She had nothing to do with the lie."

"Oh, Oliver," his mother said, bringing her hands to her cheeks.

"I haven't been honest with you," Oliver said, looking around the room. "And I've made a lot of mistakes. But I want to make up for the wrongs I've done if I can, starting with one from the distant past."

My heart beat like crazy as he came toward me and knelt down at my feet. This time, he took my hand, and slid his grandmother's ring off my finger. "It's not that I don't want you to have this," he said. "I do. But I need to earn that privilege first, and it's going to take a little more time."

He pocketed the ring and looked over his shoulder at his grandmother. "If it's okay with you, Gran, I'll hold onto it."

She nodded her consent.

Oliver focused on me again. Reaching into his other pocket, he pulled out … a Tamagotchi.

I'm not even kidding, he pulled out a fucking Tamagotchi.

"Chloe, this is something I've owed you for a long time. It's a symbol of one of the first times I let you down."

I started to cry. I couldn't help it.

"I know it doesn't make up for the pain I've caused you, but I hope you'll see it as a new beginning for us—a nod to our past *and* our future."

"I don't know what to say," I wept.

"Say yes. Say you'll give me another chance. I promise, in front of all these people"—he gestured around the room—"who will hold me to account, no more games. I want the real thing."

"Me too, Oliver. But I'm scared." I felt heat in my face and knew it had to be beet red. "And this is really sweet with the Tamagotchi and all, but you're totally putting me on the spot here."

"I'm sorry. But I wanted you to be here when I told my family the truth. I wanted you to hear me say publicly that I'm sorry for what I put you through, and even though you have every right to walk away from me, I hope you'll stay."

I was so tempted to give in immediately and say *yes, of course I'll stay*. After all, I was crazy about him and wanted him in my life. But he needed to know I would not be taken for granted or made to feel foolish again. "Could we maybe have a few minutes alone?" I asked quietly.

"Absolutely," said Aunt Nell, rising quickly to her feet. "Dinner is ready, everyone. Why don't we go into the dining room and be seated? Chloe and Oliver, you can join us whenever you're ready."

"Thanks, Mom," Oliver said, rising to his feet.

"And if you screw this up, you're grounded," she whispered ferociously before rounding everyone up and herding them out of the library.

Then we were alone.

Oliver sat next to me on the couch and handed me the Tamagotchi. "Here. This is for you. And I'm sorry I ambushed you in front of everyone again."

I smiled tightly. "You like a show. I know this about you."

"You know me better than anyone."

Nodding slowly, I took a deep breath and looked at the Tamagotchi in my hands. "I want to believe everything you're saying. And I want us to be together. I want to trust you. But this is hard for me."

"I know."

"It means a lot that you told your family the truth. That couldn't have been easy."

"You know what?" Oliver thought for a moment. "It kind of was. Or maybe not easy, but once I'd made the decision, it felt good to get all that off my chest. Like unloading a lot of old baggage before starting a new journey." He took my hands. "Come with me. I don't know exactly where we go from here or if we can get the money for that land or not, but even if we can't—I don't care. You're more important to me than any real estate or business deal or dollar amount."

Joy squeezed my heart. "I love hearing that."

"I realized today when I was out on the water that none of it would matter if I didn't have you by my side. I wouldn't even want that stupid farm."

I had to laugh. "You're not supposed to lie to me, remember?"

"I'm serious." He tucked my hair behind my ear and tipped up my chin. "I love you, Chloe. It's okay if you don't believe me, or if you don't love me back. I'm still going to love you."

I tilted my cheek against his palm. "You know I love you. I've always loved you—well, *mostly*. When you weren't pranking me or calling me chicken or betting I wasn't brave enough to jump off a roof."

"I take it all back." He pressed his lips to mine. "You're the bravest person I know. And I'm sorry you broke your leg."

"I'm sorry you broke your collarbone. But you *were* kind of an idiot to jump after you saw how badly I'd landed."

"Well, I couldn't let you best me," he said, looking and sounding like his eleven-year-old self again. "I wouldn't have been able to live with myself. And besides." He grabbed me and pulled me across his lap, tipping his forehead to mine. "You jump, I jump. Always."

I smiled. "Always."

Twenty-Five

Oliver

NOW

WE WALKED OUT OF THE LIBRARY AND INTO THE dining room hand in hand. Everyone was seated at the table already, and they must have been talking about us, because conversation came to a halt the moment we appeared.

"Everything okay?" my mother asked nervously, setting down her fork. The food on her plate—on everyone's plates—was untouched.

"Everything is okay," I said.

She looked at Chloe for confirmation.

"Everything is okay," Chloe echoed.

"Oh, thank goodness." My mother leaned back in her seat, hand on her chest.

I elbowed Chloe. "She never could resist me."

My mother rolled her eyes. "Good grief, Oliver. Behave yourself. You're barely out of hot water with Chloe as it is."

"I'm used to him by now," Chloe said. "Sorry to hold up dinner."

"Don't worry about it," my dad said. "Glad you kids have worked things out. And tomorrow, son, we're going to have a talk about work ethic and strength of character. You've got some explaining to do."

"Uh, sure thing, Dad." I pulled out Chloe's chair for her and took my seat, trying to think of a way to avoid my father's insufferable work ethic lecture. I'd heard it at least a million times growing up. Clearly I'd have to do better with my own kids. Or come up with one that was even more torturous.

The thought actually made me smile. I could see myself being that dad one day.

And I saw Chloe by my side. It was the first time being a husband and father hadn't seemed like something I had to do because it was expected—it was something I wanted to do.

"So what will you do about the land you planned to buy for the rye?" my brother asked. Of course.

I tried not to let it bother me as I spread my napkin on my lap. "I'll apply for a loan, I guess. If it's meant to be, it'll be."

"Just a minute."

Everyone looked at Gran.

She rose to her feet at one end of the table. "It seems there's still a business opportunity to be had here. And as I'm ninety, I feel like my time to invest in talented entrepreneurs might be running out."

I shook my head. "Thanks, Gran, but I've decided I want to do this on my own."

"I'm not talking about you. I'm talking about Chloe."

My jaw dropped. Everyone's jaw dropped.

"What do you mean?" Charlotte asked.

"I mean, I'm going to invest a million dollars in Chloe. What she chooses to do with it, and whom she chooses to share it with, is her business. But she impresses me. She's got heart and smarts and moxie, and it doesn't get better than that."

We all looked at Chloe. Her face was white as a sheet. I glanced back at Gran, and she winked at me.

I smiled back, appreciating what she was doing for me.

"What do you say, Chloe?" Gran asked. "Will you accept my offer to invest in your future?"

Chloe met my eyes and I shrugged. "Your decision. No pressure here."

"This is insane!" she cried, laughing and wiping tears from her eyes. "A million dollars?"

"A million dollars." Gran's eyes glittered. "And maybe a bottle of that fancy whiskey you're going to make."

"Deal," Chloe said, putting her hand on her chest. "Oh my God, my heart is racing so fast. I can't believe this! Thank you!"

"You're welcome. I have the utmost faith in you." She looked at me and smiled. "In both of you."

"Thank you, Gran," I said, my throat tight. "That means a lot to us."

"Chloe is going to be a busy woman," said her father.

We all looked at Uncle John.

"I am?" asked Chloe.

"Yes." He put his arm around his wife and looked at his daughter. "Your mother has finally convinced me to retire this fall, and the only person I trust to run Cloverleigh is you. You've been there longer than anyone and know the place inside and out. You work hard, you work smart. You've got the education, the experience, the work ethic, the gut instincts, and the passion it takes."

"But what about April?" Chloe asked.

Her mother smiled. "April is happy doing what she does. She's one hundred percent on board with you taking over as COO. Everyone is—Sylvia, April, Meg, Frannie, Mack, Henry … if you want the job, it's yours."

I found myself getting choked up and grabbed Chloe's hand.

"This is all so surreal," she said, blinking back tears. "I feel like everything is happening at once."

"Do you need some time to think things through?" her mom asked.

"No!" Chloe burst out. "When have I ever taken time to think things through? I want the job—give it to me!"

Everyone laughed and I kissed her cheek. "Congratulations. We will make this work, I promise. You'll be busy, but you can do it."

"Thank you," she said breathlessly, squeezing my hand.

"Well, hear, hear!" my father said, raising his glass. "A toast to new beginnings!"

My mother quickly poured wine for Chloe and me. "A toast to a wonderful past."

"To love and family," said Aunt Daphne with shining eyes.

"To friends who *are* family," said Uncle John.

Chloe lifted her glass. "To second chances."

I leaned toward her. "I might need more than that."

"I might give them," she teased.

We locked eyes as we drank to our past, our present, and our future.

Later that night, we undressed and climbed into bed. I wrapped my arms around her beneath the covers. "I can't believe I almost lost you again."

"Me neither." She snuggled up tight, her head on my chest. "That was a close call."

"I'm going to try really hard to be the man you deserve, Chloe. I mean that."

"All I want is you." She kissed my bare chest. "And you don't have to be perfect. Just honest."

"I will be. For example, I'm honestly thinking that I'd really like to have sex with you right now."

Giggling, she shook her head. "No way. Your parents, *my* parents, your grandmother, your nephews—they're all right down the hall. And this old bed squeaks."

"So let's do it on the floor."

"The floors in this house creak more than the beds!"

I sighed. "You're really going to make me wait until we get home to be inside you again?"

"Sorry. Yes." She was silent for a moment. "So where will home be?"

"Where do you want it to be?"

She picked up her head and looked at me. "Honestly?"

I flicked her earlobe. "Duh."

"Right at Cloverleigh."

"Then it will be home to me too."

Her smile lit up the dark. "You mean it?"

"Sure. I'll get a condo in Traverse, or buy a little house in Hadley Harbor. I've never lived small town life. Maybe it will suit me."

"I hope so." She brushed her fingertips across my collarbone. "Or you could stay with me at Cloverleigh if you want. Even if it's just temporary."

"Chloe, if I move in with you, I'm never going to want to leave."

"Really?"

"Really. I mean, you'll be there all the time cooking for me, doing my laundry, ironing my shirts—"

She smacked me on the chest. "Very funny."

"I'm teasing." Grabbing her arms, I flipped her onto her back. Kissed her lips. "I'm never going to want to leave because I love you. And I want to spend the rest of my life with you. There's nothing I don't want to share, and I can't believe I wasted so much time." I kissed her again. "I don't want to waste any more."

Slipping her arms free, she looped them around my neck and wrapped her legs around me. "You're making me want to risk the squeaky bed," she whispered.

"We could." I moved my mouth across her cheek to her ear. "Or we could go into my closet, where I first kissed you."

She went completely still. "You remember."

"Of course I remember. Who forgets their first kiss?"

"It wasn't really a kiss."

I pulled back and looked down at her. "Um, our lips touched. Also our tongues."

"And we decided it was so disgusting, we'd never kiss anyone else again."

"We were pretty young." I pictured her at that age—pigtailed and gap-toothed. Dimpled cheeks.

"We had to be, what, six?" she wondered.

"If that."

She laughed. "I never told a soul about it."

"Me neither. I think I tried to block it entirely from my memory. I was so grossed out."

"And yet it was your idea," she said.

"No, it wasn't. It was yours."

"No way." She shook her head. "You brought it up. I'm positive."

"I might have brought it up, but you suggested we do it."

"I did not!"

"How about we agree to disagree? After all, there's no way to know for sure, and you and I will argue forever." I slanted my mouth over hers again, stroking her tongue with mine. "But I definitely think we need a new memory for that closet."

"You didn't put a rubber snake in there, did you?"

"No. But I do have a one-eyed trouser—"

"No snake jokes, please. Especially if you're trying to turn me on."

"Is that a yes to the closet?"

"You know me," she whispered, reaching between us to stroke my erection. "I've always loved trouble."

In the end, we didn't make it to the closet, and the bed made a horrendous amount of noise. I convinced Chloe our parents deserved it for throwing us together so much, and Gran was ninety and hard of hearing anyway.

Afterward, as we snuggled up again beneath the blankets, I had to laugh.

"What's funny?" she asked, stifling a yawn.

"Everything. This. Us. The fact that twenty-some years ago we were sitting in that closet over there swearing we'd never kiss anyone again, let alone each other."

"It is pretty amazing. We've come a long way. It makes me happy to think of it."

I kissed the top of her head. "Me too. You think if we could go back in time and tell those two kids in the closet what would happen in the future they'd believe us?"

She laughed and cuddled closer. "Not a chance."

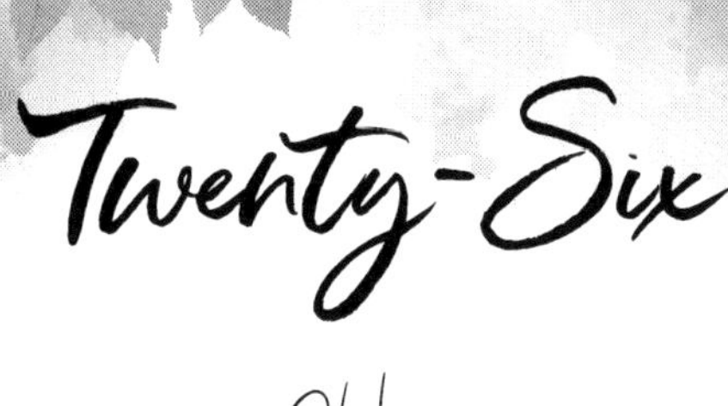

Twenty-Six

Chloe

THEN

"HAVE YOU EVER TOUCHED TONGUES WITH anyone?" Oliver asked.

We were six, sitting cross-legged on the floor of his closet, hiding so we didn't have to go downstairs for dinner. We had a giant bag of Better Made potato chips, a couple cans of Vernor's ginger ale, a box of chocolate covered strawberries, and a thick slice of maple fudge. We figured that was all the food groups. The closet door was shut, but thankfully we had a flashlight, which threw a cone of light at the ceiling.

"Ew, no," I said, crunching on a chip. "Have you?"

"No." He slurped from his can of Vernor's and then burped.

Boys were so gross.

"But I've seen it," he went on. "On a TV show."

"Was it grown ups?" I asked.

"It was, like, teenagers," he said.

"Huh." I ate another chip. "Is that what teenagers do?"

"I think so." He munched on the fudge, taking a bite out of the slab. "Want some?"

"Sure."

Oliver broke off a piece and handed it to me. As it dissolved in my mouth, I started thinking about what another person's tongue would actually taste like. "I wonder what it's like. Touching tongues with someone."

"Me too."

"It's probably really disgusting, but maybe we should try it. Then we'd know for sure."

"Okay. Stick out your tongue."

"Hold on. I have to swallow." I took a drink of ginger ale. "Now I'm ready."

Squeezing my eyes shut, I stuck my tongue out and waited as Oliver leaned toward me, presumably with his tongue out too. But he missed my mouth and ended up licking my cheek.

"Gross," I said, wiping my cheek with my sleeve.

"Sorry, my eyes were closed. I'll try again."

I shut mine again, and suddenly I felt his hands on my shoulders and his lips touching mine. He hadn't left me any time to prepare! Quickly I poked my tongue between our lips and he did the same. His was warm and firm and I could sort of taste ginger ale. Altogether the sensation was pretty slimy and disgusting.

After less than half a second, we broke apart.

"Ew," we both said at the same time.

He wiped his tongue with the bottom of his T-shirt.

I licked my sleeve to get rid of his spit. "That was *blech*. I'm never doing that again."

"Me neither."

With that decided, we went back to eating our snacks.

"Even if I get married, if my husband wants to kiss, I'm saying no," I announced.

Oliver snorted. "Don't worry, no one will want to marry you."

"No one will want to marry you, either," I told him.

"Good. Girls are stupid."

"*You're* stupid."

"At least I'm not a chicken."

"I'm not a chicken!"

At that moment, the door to the closet flew open and our mothers stood there with their hands on their hips. "There you are!" Aunt Nell shouted. "We've been looking everywhere."

"You're late for dinner," my mother added. "And what's all that junk you're eating?"

"Whose idea was this?" Aunt Nell crossed her arms and tapped her toe. "Oliver? Chloe? I'm listening."

Oliver and I exchanged a look, during which we tacitly agreed not to tattle on each other. We were both at fault—it had been his idea to skip dinner and mine to raid the pantry.

"Come out of that closet right now," my mom demanded. "And go clean up for dinner."

Without another word, we scrambled to our feet and hurried to do as we were told.

We didn't get dessert that night, which was a bummer because it was Sander's hot fudge cream puffs, my favorite. "Maybe next time, you two will think twice before disobeying the rules," said Aunt Nell.

Oliver and I exchanged another look that said *not a chance*.

We might not have liked kissing, we might not have even liked *each other* that much, but one thing we did like was disobeying the rules.

Needless to say, there were many nights Oliver and I went without dessert. We never could stay out of trouble. But with one look across the dinner table, I always knew he was thinking the same thing I was.

Worth it.

It's what made us so undeniably good together.

Always.

Epilogue

Chloe

Late August

"OLIVER, THIS IS INSANE. WHY DO I HAVE TO KEEP my eyes closed?" I moved forward with halting steps, both my hands in his, like awkward middle schoolers at a dance. We were in the hallway outside my office at Cloverleigh—well, our office. We shared it now, in addition to sharing my Traverse City condo and his apartment in Detroit, which we'd decided to keep for the time being, since we'd be down there a lot. I was learning everything I could about the distilling process at Brown Eyed Girl, and when we were at Cloverleigh, I was trailing my father a lot, learning everything I'd need to know when he retired for good this fall. He and my mother were leaving for a cruise around the world in October—right after Frannie and Mack's wedding.

It meant Oliver and I were together nearly twenty-four seven, but neither of us was complaining. In fact, I was happier than I'd ever been. We both were.

"You have to keep your eyes closed because I want to surprise you," he said.

"I don't like surprises."

"Hush. Don't you have any sense of romance? Hold on, I'm opening the door."

"I can't think about romance!" I exclaimed as I let him lead me outside into the heat of a hot summer day. "We were supposed to leave for South Manitou by one. If we wait much longer, we won't catch the afternoon ferry."

"So we'll go in the morning. I talked to the Feldmanns and they said they'll be working sunup to sundown." He continued walking backward with his hands holding mine.

"But I told you I wanted to be there for the very first planting," I complained. "We're missing a priceless opportunity for photos to use on social media."

"I promise you we will have all the social media photos you need. We'll get up early and catch the first ferry and spend all day in your million-dollar fields, whispering sweet nothings to our rye seeds."

I laughed. "They're not *my* million-dollar fields. They're ours."

"So you say. Come this way."

I made a half turn as he indicated. Keeping my eyes closed, I listened carefully. Sniffed the fecund air. "Are we on the path to the barn?"

"Good guess. But the question is, *why* are we on the path to the barn?"

"I have no idea, Oliver. You tell me."

"It has to do with the date."

"The date?" I thought for a moment. It was August thirtieth … was it supposed to mean something? "I don't get it. It's no one's birthday, it's not a holiday, it's not an anniversary."

"But it is." Gently he led me into the barn and across the hay-strewn, wooden-planked floor.

My mind was spinning. An anniversary? He and I hadn't been together long enough to have an anniversary. It hadn't even been two full months. Granted, things couldn't be better between us, and our story had started long before he—

It hit me, and I gasped. "Oh my God. Is it?"

"Is it what?" His voice held a smile.

"The anniversary of the jump?"

"Good thinking. You can open your eyes to climb the ladder."

I opened them to find him standing next to the ladder leading to the loft. His blue eyes danced with mischief, and his grin was devious as hell. My heart thumped hard a few times—it felt like a warning. "Oliver, what is this? Tell me before I go up there."

He laughed and slapped my butt. "Chicken. Climb up."

With an exasperated sigh, I started up the ladder. Oliver followed, and from the loft we climbed onto the roof.

Immediately Oliver took my hand. "Careful," he said. "Come this way."

Slowly, we walked over to the edge of the roof where he'd issued the challenge. Then he turned to face me and took the other hand.

"So," he said. "Here we are again."

"Are you going to dare me to jump?"

"No, but I am going to ask you to take a leap with me."

My heart stopped. "What?"

Oliver dropped to one knee. "I was trying to get the timing exactly right. According to my mother's—and your mother's—memories, it was around two in the afternoon when we made that fateful bet."

I laughed and nodded, but my throat was so tight I couldn't speak.

"I know I screwed up, proposing to you at the cottage like that. It was out of nowhere, it was too rushed, it was too public. And I went into it for the wrong reasons. But when I took the ring back, it wasn't because I didn't love you enough, or I didn't want to spend the rest of my life with you. Because I do."

A tear slipped down my cheek, and I sniffed.

"At the time, I promised myself I'd never make that kind of mistake again. I wouldn't rush things or be selfish. I vowed I would be patient and give you all the time you needed to trust me again, to believe in me. To know without a doubt that you are everything good in my life." He reached into his pocket and pulled out Gran's ring. "But again—I lied."

I sniffled and smiled. "You did?"

He nodded. "Yes. Because when it comes to you, I can't be patient. I know what I want, and I want it now. And if that makes me sound like a spoiled brat, well, it wouldn't be the first time you called me that name. And probably not the last."

Tears fell faster now, but I was laughing too. "Probably not."

He turned my hand over and slid the ring on my finger, then looked up at me. The afternoon sun made his blue eyes look light and clear, and his skin golden. "Marry me, Chloe. I want you to be my wife. I want to be your husband. I want to be partners in everything—our business, our marriage, our family. I want a house that's just ours. I don't care where, I don't care what size, I only care that I live in it with you and our unbelievably beautiful and smart but completely disobedient kids who are going to try to get away with breaking every rule, just like their parents did."

"Oh God, they're going to be terrible, aren't they?" I asked, laughing through tears. But I couldn't stop staring at the ring on my finger.

"Probably. But we'll survive. And we'll be happy." He squeezed my hand. "So come on, Dimples. Say yes. I dare you."

I dropped to my knees too, taking his face in my hands. "Yes," I said through joyful tears. "Yes!"

We kissed quickly, then Oliver leaned slightly toward the edge of the roof. "She said yes!" he shouted.

Immediately I heard cheers and applause from down below. Open-mouthed, I walked nearer to the edge and saw almost my entire family—and his—gathered below. My parents, April, Mack and Frannie and all three of the girls, Aunt Nell, Uncle Soapy, Gran, Hughie and Lisa and their boys. Even Charlotte was there with Guy and their brand new baby. I smiled and waved. "I said yes! It's for real this time!"

"Come down for champagne!" April called.

"But take the ladder!" my mother yelled frantically. "No jumping!"

Oliver and I laughed and held hands as we carefully walked back toward the loft. Once we were safely off the roof and inside the barn, I couldn't resist throwing my arms around him again. He wrapped me up in his embrace and spun me around, my heels in the air.

Laughing, I buried my face in his neck. "I never want my feet to touch the ground, Oliver."

"Good," he said. "Because this leap goes on forever."

The End

Also by Melanie Harlow

The Frenched Series

Frenched

Yanked

Forked

Floored

The Happy Crazy Love Series

Some Sort of Happy

Some Sort of Crazy

Some Sort of Love

The After We Fall Series

Man Candy

After We Fall

If You Were Mine

From This Moment

The One and Only Series

Only You

Only Him

Only Love

THE CLOVERLEIGH FARMS SERIES

Irresistible

Undeniable

Hold You Close (Co-written with Corinne Michaels)

Imperfect Match (Co-written with Corinne Michaels)

Strong Enough

(A M/M romance co-written with David Romanov)

The Speak Easy Duet

The Tango Lesson (A Standalone Novella

Acknowledgments

Much love and gratitude to the following people!

Melissa Gaston, Brandi Zelenka, Jenn Watson, Hang Le, Kayti McGee, Laurelin Paige, Sierra Simone, Lauren Blakely, Corinne Michaels, Sarah Ferguson and the entire Social Butterfly dream team, Rebecca Friedman at Friedman Literary, Flavia Viotti at Bookcase Literary, Nancy Smay at Evident Ink, early readers Michele Ficht, Alison Evans-Maxwell, and Louise McKie, Stacey Blake at Champagne Book Design, Andi Arndt at Lyric Audio, narrators Stephen Dexter and Savannah Peachwood, the Shop Talkers, the Harlots and the Harlot ARC Team, bloggers and event organizers, my Queens, my readers all over the world … and always, always, always my family. I love you.

About the Author

Melanie Harlow likes her heels high, her martini dry, and her history with the naughty bits left in. In addition to The Cloverleigh Farms Series, she's the author of the One and Only Series, the After We Fall Series, the Happy Crazy Love Series, the Frenched Series, *Hold You Close* and *Imperfect Match* (co-authored with Corinne Michaels), *Strong Enough* (a M/M romance co-authored with David Romanov), and *The Speak Easy Duet* (a historical romance set in the 1920s). She writes from her home outside of Detroit, where she lives with her husband and two daughters. When she's not writing, she's probably got a cocktail in hand. And sometimes when she is.

Find her here …

Website® www.melanieharlow.com
Newsletter®harlow.pub/mh-news
Amazon®harlow.pub/amazon
Instagram® @melanie_harlow
Bookbub®harlow.pub/bb
Facebook Reader Group® Harlow's Harlots

Made in the USA
Columbia, SC
13 August 2023

21568601R00159